I stared appraisingly at the redhead curled up on my couch. Even she, Laurie Hendricks, might be one of them—one of the things from outer space.

She noticed me watching her. She smiled knowingly, and stretched, catlike, her body straining against the smooth coverall.

She walked over to where I stood and pressed against me. "Let's see what you can teach me, professor," she said softly.

My last thought was: This girl is flesh and blood and human—she *must* be human! And then everything was blotted out in the crimson sensation of that incredible kiss. . . .

A Zenith Original

Louis Charbonneau

CORPUS
EARTHLING

Zenith Books, Inc.
Rockville Centre, New York

1

IT CAME AGAIN—the dream within a dream, the alien mind within the ailing mind. Drowning in the treacherous whirlpool near the shores of sleep, I fought to reach the firm reality of consciousness, of awakening, but I was sucked back and slowly sank beneath the surface into the horror of the dream. . . .

I stood on a lonely stretch of beach in a blue night, the sand glistening white against the inky darkness of sky and water. Waves rolled and tumbled toward me in noisy confusion. Beyond the apron of sand were the small, black beetle-shapes of a cluster of house trailers. But my eyes were focused on the figure which stood far up the beach, and an unknown terror crawled like a furry, many-legged animal down the nape of my neck.

"No!" The wind snatched the single cry of protest from my lips and tore it into thin shreds of sound.

And the alien mind spoke in my ear, in my mind but not of it, a whispered insinuation. "Drown!" it urged. "Drown!"

I didn't move. My legs seemed to have grown into the sand like the trunks of trees. The voice spoke again in my mind, louder, more compelling.

"Walk! Now! Into the water!"

I stood resisting the terrifying power of the voice. The figure up the beach seemed closer, blurred by the cold wind that brought tears to my eyes. I stood rooted and my body bent as if a gale a tugged and pulled at it. My legs began to tremble uncontrollably. The command hammered at me with a relentless pressure, filling my mind, blotting out all consciousness save for the drumming words, overwhelming in their brutal strength.

And one foot moved. I took a step. Awkwardly, stiffly, like a rusty robot lifting its leg. I struggled to force my body to obey the protest of my own will. No! Stop! Don't move! But the cry of resistance was obliterated by the command that swelled within my brain.

"Walk! Walk! Walk!"

Feet dragged resisting in the soft sand. Then there was the packed wet surface, dark footprints, and the cold spray against my face, the water swirling around my ankles, receding rapidly away from me down the wet brown slope. I stumbled after it, impelled by the irresistible force, each step a painful conflict that racked my body. I flung a wild glance toward the figure on the beach. Closer now, much closer. Moving in for the kill. And I felt anger, raging helpless anger mixed with the terror.

A breaker cracked like a whip ahead of me. The foaming tail of the wave tumbled and crashed around me, washing above my knees. For a single moment, I braked to a stop. I could feel the fabric of my suit plastered wet against my legs.

I fought again and lost.

Walk. Drown. One step, then another. The water waist-high, dragging against my thighs, a numbing cold. A breaker rising, trembling at its crest, smashing down to drive me off my feet, tumbling me helplessly in the churning violence.

"Up! On your feet! Walk!"

Eyelids heavy and wet, the salt taste on my tongue. The cold, bone deep. Staggering, half falling, dragging myself forward against the pull of the water. Another breaker, and I fell face forward into it. My whole body was numb and wet and shivering, and the chill penetrated my brain where the voice pounded at me with its relentless power, shattering my will, dominating me as if I were a simple-minded child, driving me onward step by step. Another wave broke over me, lifting me off my feet and slamming me back, the water filling eyes and nose and mouth as I went under.

6

I swallowed water and came up choking with a heavy pain in my chest.

"Drown! Drown!"

The voice spoke pitilessly and I staggered forward once more. And at last I was beyond the line of the breakers, out where the water rose with a slow heaviness, building high behind me. And there was a new strength in the deep pull of the water flowing out to sea. Another step, another, still one more. And I tried to ask why, but my brain would not function. The water rose above my head and I went down, down, sinking into the cold black waters.

The voice was triumphant, exulting, reaching through the tumultuous sea to the numbness of my brain. "Now drown! Give yourself to the water! Die!"

In the last moment panic came—the body retching, trying to disgorge the deadly water, the mind recoiling from the black abyss that beckoned, now so near, so tempting. And I tried to push up from the bottom of the sea, but the water was a thick, impenetrable wall toppling down upon me. I could see a layer of light near the surface and I strained frantically to reach it, to grope beyond it toward the life-giving air. The alien mind which had driven me under was now—

The mind was silent.

I woke shivering in my bed. The sheets were damp with sweat. I lay rigid, unable to move. The panic drained out slowly. I thought of nothing, staring dully at the sleek surface of the plastic ceiling overhead. When at last the terror had ebbed away, I felt empty and cold and spent, as if all strength and sinew had rushed out through the opening where the fear had gone.

A dream, I told myself. Only a dream. But the feeble reassurance carried no conviction. The barrier against thought which I had erected gave way, and the chill knowledge of what was happening to me spilled through the breach to strike with sickening impact.

I was going mad.

7

2

I ROSE SLOWLY. The muscles of arms and legs and shoulders felt stiff and sore, as if they had actually been tested and strained in the ordeal of which I had dreamt. I glanced at the luminous clock face built into the wall just to the left of the bedroom telescreen. It was after three in the morning.

The floor of the trailer creaked gently as I plodded barefoot into the tiny kitchenette. The creak always gave me the impression that the trailer was moving, like a ship that groans protestingly even as it rides with no apparent sway on smooth waters. I pressed the coffee button and then, because I was too tired to move into the living area when I would only have to come back in a minute, I stood beside the sink, staring at the glowing red button as if hypnotized by it. I couldn't shake off the depression brought by the recurrence of the dream.

The red button blinked off, a green one flared, and a coffee cup dropped into the slot beneath the spout from which coffee poured in a hot black stream. I added a sugar pill and carried the cup into the living room.

This was a small room about seven feet wide and ten feet long. All of the furniture was built in—a sofa across the narrow wall under the picture window, two flanking plastic chairs on pedestal bases, a coffee table and a desk with its contour pedestal stool. Cramped quarters, but they were comfortable enough for one. The kitchenette in the center of the trailer had a small dining area. Beyond it were the bath, utility closets, and the small bedroom. I had never completely got over my luck in finding a place so close to the university.

Particularly one with a view.

I pressed the wall button and the draperies parted slowly and silently across the picture window to frame a panoramic view of the west basin of the San Fernando Valley. It was a clear moonlit night. The trailer community I lived in was on a knoll above Mulholland Drive near the crest of the Santa Monica mountains. Behind me, at the southern foot of the hills, were the massive buildings of the University of California at Los Angeles. My trailer faced northwest. In the distance I could see the glow which was always visible over the spaceport of the Western Space Command, though I could not now make out the bullet-shaped noses of the shuttle rockets pointing skyward, dominant landmarks which could easily be seen in the daytime projecting above an intervening ridge of hills at the far western end of the valley. The ever-present glow came from the atomic reactor factory where the power plants were produced for the interplanetary space ships. These days the bullet-nosed rockets were thundering skyward daily, carrying parts to the space station where the interplanetary ships were being assembled.

Thinking of the coming moment less than a month away when man would be leaving on his second flight to Mars, I felt some of my depression lifting. The good hot coffee had quieted the quivering muscles in my stomach. I lit a cigarette and inhaled deeply.

At last I permitted my mind to return to the dream. It was the third time I had experienced it, the same dream in every detail, with its latent death wish, its peculiar delusion of extraordinary mental powers, its mysterious unknown enemy, its strange water fear. The terrifying reality of the dream, coupled with the unshakable conviction that it was in some way a portent, only partly explained why it left me so shaken.

For the dream was not the only sympton I had had. There were also the voices—and the clear sense of someone plotting against me. Sometimes the voices were extraordinarily vivid, whispering in my ear with as much clarity as if I were wearing earphones and tuning in a broadcast. I would stand at the window overlooking the valley, or even in my cubicle of an office at the university, and I would hear the meaningless fragments of thought—phrases, words and half-words jumping into my mind with an eerie suddenness, bringing the peculiar sensation that the thoughts in my own mind were being formed by someone else. For over a year I had heard the elusive voices, but it wa~ only recently that I had begun to entertain the deli~ that they were plotting against me.

"Someone is listening."

That startling declaration had chilled my mind a little over a month ago. There had been an immediate impression of total silence, of waiting in a mental vacuum, and I had found myself holding my breath, my mind blank in readiness. But there had been nothing else—only the waiting silence.

In the weeks that followed, the references to the listener —to me, I was sure—had been numerous. And I had sensed a deep animosity toward me in the voices that spoke to me unknowingly. They were trying to locate me. Who they were, I had no idea. But they were hunting me coldly and methodically.

In the dream they caught me.

Psychology was not my field. I taught English literature at the university and I was more familiar with Dostoyevsky's probing of the human mind than Jung's or Freud's. But after I started hearing the voices, I did some intensive reading on abnormal psychology. I even quizzed friends in the psychology department, being careful not to discuss my symptoms with them openly.

The research had been frightening. I had found nothing in the literature of psychology that exactly duplicated my symptoms—but I learned that minds, like fingerprints, always had their individual twists. And there were man~ parallels to my particular pattern, cases of multiple pers~ ality in which one identity had spoken to the other as a clear voice in the mind—and had even tried to "murder" his fellow. The conflict of personalities often expressed itself in dreams in which the unconscious mind cleverly dramatized the conflict in bizarre terms. The fact that the

10

enemy on the beach was unrecognizable was even a typical factor.

I knew that I should have treatment while there was still time—before I did something dangerous. It was not beyond the area of possibility that I would try to kill myself as the dream suggested. And yet—

I believed in the voices. Reason said they could not exist. Logic argued that they were products of my own ailing mind. But my belief in them was a barrier that prevented me from seeking treatment at once. I kept searching for explanations of the voices. I kept thinking of them as completely foreign to me. I built up a flimsy case for the actual existence of beings who were telepathic, who communicated by direct thought transference. They were engaged in some melodramatic plot. Against whom? Me, of course. But only because I was a menace. I was able to hear them. I was a threat to some kind of monstrous plot that was far bigger than me, far more important than my life.

I found it easier to demolish these theories than to construct them; nevertheless I clung to them with a desperate hope. For either there were real voices, there were real enemies, or I was insane.

These brooding reflections were interrupted by a splash of light that fell across the narrow strip of lawn outside my trailer. I crossed quickly to the side window and peered through the vertical plastic blinds. When I saw the source of the light I relaxed, smiling faintly. For a moment I continued to stare at the curtained bedroom window of the adjoining trailer. This time I could see nothing clearly, only a blurred shadow of movement. It was enough to recreate a vivid picture. A moment later, light glowed at the front of the trailer, but again the blinds cut me off from my neighbor.

With a slight feeling of embarrassment I turned away, remembering the guilt I had felt a few nights before when my new neighbor had forgotten to draw her bedroom curtains closed. There is something especially stimulating in seeing a beautiful woman when she isn't aware of being observed. And in this case nothing had prepared me for the golden grace of the girl's figure.

She had moved into the adjoining trailer only two weeks before. Trailer life is of necessity fairly intimate and I had met her briefly a number of times. She was not the kind of girl you particularly notice. I had got the impression that she was painfully shy. The first time I met her, the day after she moved in, I said hello casually. She blurted a reply, stammered a name I didn't catch when I introduced myself, whirled, and fled into her trailer. I failed to get a clear impression of what she looked like. Young. Slender. Taller than average. Blonde. Not a real yellow or a striking white-blonde, but fair. Large, frightened eyes whose color I hadn't caught. And that's all. Nothing that would enable me to recognize her on the street.

During the days that followed, she avoided close contact. My first instinctive suspicion of any newcomer, a reaction to the knowledge that I was being hunted by an unknown enemy, quickly evaporated. I exchanged greetings with the girl a couple of times, but she didn't invite conversation and passed on quickly. I concluded that she would probably misinterpret any friendly overtures I made and I dismissed her as a timid soul who wanted to be left alone. I wasn't interested.

Until that midnight glimpse through the bedroom window. Glancing out, I had been startled by the extraordinary sight of the girl in the act of pulling a nightgown over her head. Too surprised to move, I stopped to gape at her. The gown was a pale iridescent green against the honey tones of her skin. For several seconds she stood completely revealed, her arms raised, small breasts pulled tautly erect, her body bathed in soft light. Then she lowered her arms and took a step forward which placed her out of my line of sight. I became rudely aware of what I was doing. Chagrined, I told myself to stop acting like a peeping Tom, but I couldn't erase that golden image from my memory. It gave me a restless night.

Now, with a somewhat rueful smile, I turned out the lights in the front of my trailer and went back to the small bedroom. I felt a return attack of nerves at the prospect of going to sleep again. Perchance to dream. Ay, there's the rub. For in that sleep of sleeps what dreams may come . . .

I forced myself to turn out the light and lie on the narrow bed. After a while my eyes began to ache from the effort of staring at the ceiling. Don't think about it, I told myself. You've never had the dream twice in one night. You can think about it tomorrow. In the daylight. Think of the girl next door. You forgot all about your troubles when you glanced out the window.

Maybe sex is your whole problem. How would a psycho-analyst interpret your dream? The faceless enemy is obvious. That means it's someone very close to you, someone you hate but shouldn't hate—or someone for whom you feel a forbidden love. And what about the water symbol?

But there was no one very close to me, no one it could have been. My mother was dead. Over two years. And I had never known my father, the man from Los Alamitos who had been my mother's lover for a week in Albuquerque and had left his seed in her.

And it was an answer, of course. The bastard son. What was the ratio of insanity among bastards? Higher than normal? I would have to look it up.

I shut the thought out of my mind. For a long while, I stared at the dim whiteness of the plastic ceiling. And then the picture of a shy, fair-haired girl with firm, uplifted breasts stole into my thoughts. The tension slid away from me. The horror of the dream was forgotten.

It's funny, the tricks your mind can play on you.

3

THE FOLLOWING NIGHT I worked late, correcting a batch of the interminable freshman themes. I didn't have any night classes, but the offices were bright for the lecturers who did. I found it difficult to concentrate on the semi-adolescent exercises in expository composition even though the office was quiet and almost empty most of the evening. Near the bottom of the pile of papers I came across one theme that jolted me. It was called "How to Conduct a Seance." It was a juvenile and jocular approach to the subject, and I had never placed much credence myself in preternatural events and influences—or in extra-sensory powers. But now I found myself feeling defensive, resenting the spoofing tone of the student's theme. Wasn't anything possible? How much did we really know? Wasn't the wisest philosopher actually as ignorant as this nineteen-year-old?

I wondered if a man could have unusual perceptions, strange mental powers, for twenty-seven years without knowing it. Wouldn't a talent for thought transference or for hearing the mental communications of others make itself known early? Or would it be necessary to have two sensitive people involved, sender and receiver? Could you be a telepath without knowing it simply because you had never encountered another?

And I remembered the incident, distant in time and dim in memory, which I had refused to recall during the disturbing recent months. In itself, the experience, though startling at the time, was not unique. At least you hear about similar things happening to a great many ordinary people. You hear about it—but you brush off the story as coincidence or as the product of an over-active imagination.

14

I have mentioned my father. Until I was eighteen, I never knew who he was or that he was alive. My mother had always talked about him as if he had been killed the year I was born, during the brief Chino-American war of 1963. After I had the extraordinary vision, she told me the truth, her story muffled by tears long contained.

Ernest Cameron was a well-known physicist. He was married and had two children. If my mother can be believed, his was an unhappy marriage, but one which he did not feel justified in renouncing. During part of 1962 he was in New Mexico working with the army on atomic field weapons, the kind that did a hell of a lot of damage in a confined area, what they used to call "clean" bombs in those days before all atomic weapons were outlawed. My mother was at that time a woman in her early twenties living in Albuquerque.

She met Ernest Cameron when he was on a weekend leave. They fell in love, suddenly, catastrophically. Their passionate affair lasted for nine days. Then, as the threat of war intensified in Asia, he was abruptly transferred overseas. My mother never saw him again, but she was already carrying the infinitesimal germ of life that grew into the son he never knew. Me. Paul Cameron.

My mother always loved him. She moved to Los Angeles and took the name of Mrs. Rose Cameron, wanting me to bear my father's name. For eighteen years after I was born, she posed as a widow. The role was never questioned.

It was the vision which forced her to tell me who I really was—and who my father was. It happened on a clear sunny afternoon. I was in the yard outside our small trailer. Having just graduated from high school, I was taking a week's vacation before hunting for a job. I was sitting on a canvas chair, idly enjoying the summer sun and thinking wistfully about my hopes of going to college, when it happened.

I saw him. A sandy-haired, middle-aged man with bent, rounded shoulders and a tired walk. Preoccupied, his eyes on the ground, he stepped off a curb and started across a

15

street I had never seen in my life. I sat in the canvas chair, staring at the familiar setting of the crowded trailer court, and the picture of the sandy-haired man was superimposed on the reality before me, equally clear and vivid. When I saw the truck hurtling toward him, the illusion was so graphic that I cried out in alarm. The man looked up at the last moment of his life, soft gray eyes widening in blank surprise, without fear, as if he had not had time to bring his mind back from some distant point of reflection to this time and place of life and death. He had stepped out from behind a parked car. The truckdriver, seeing him too late, tried to swerve. There was a terrifyingly slow sequence of brakes screeching, rubber scraping off in black streaks on the pavement, big trailer lurching sideways— and the final sickening violence of impact, of smashed bones and flesh and blood.

I stood trembling beside the overturned canvas chair amid the familiar cluster of trailers and covered patios and cement walks and hotly glittering parked cars, and I knew that the echo of a final scream of pain had broken from my own lips. My mother was standing in the doorway of our trailer, her mouth open, one hand at her breast in fright, staring at me.

She ran down the steps. "Paul! My God, Paul, what happened?"

Slowly, dazedly, I looked around me. A couple of children were watching me in owlish wonder; a man had stopped some thirty yards away, staring at me over his shoulder; the woman in the next-door trailer was frozen at her window; even the birds were silent in the trees overhead. The whole world around me seemed to be arrested, waiting for me to come back to it.

My gaze shifted to my mother's face. I moved and the scene came alive again, like a motion picture that has been momentarily stopped and then resumes, the figures jumping into motion to complete the half-finished gesture, the interrupted phrase.

"I don't know," I said slowly. "I don't know."

I lit a cigarette and opened a can of beer and took a long cool drink, all the while trying to organize the confusion in my mind, trying to understand what had happened to me. My mother kept pressing me to explain what had made me cry out, and I had an impulse to assure her that it had just been a dream. It was several minutes before I felt capable of trying to put into words what I had seen. I still felt oddly detached, as if I had been away on a long trip and had only just got back so that I hadn't had time to unpack or re-orient myself to the old familiar setting.

I told her the story without softening its raw edges, quietly and dispassionately, trusting in a mother's willingness to believe that her son was neither a liar nor a madman. When I had finished I looked at her expectantly, even a little apprehensively. In the telling, the story had begun to sound fantastic. For the first time, I thought that maybe I had actually fallen asleep in the sun without realizing it and been awakened by the nightmare. But my mother's reaction was so startling that I forgot my doubts.

For several seconds, she stared at me in silence. Without warning her eyes filmed over and a tear spilled through her lashes to trickle down her cheek. In dumb fascination, I watched the slow progression of that single tear down her weathered skin.

She spoke in a strained whisper. "Would you describe him again?"

At first I didn't know what she meant. Then, puzzled, I described the man of the vision. I could see him very clearly. Sandy hair thinning over a high forehead. Soft gray eyes mirroring a compassionate intelligence. A thin, high-bridged nose. A wide, responsive mouth, curving slightly in a pensive smile. Stooped shoulders that made him look slighter and shorter than he was, though my impression was that he was taller than average.

It was only when the portrait was complete that I realized that, except for the bent shoulders and the thinning hair, I had been describing myself.

My mother looked away, covering her face with her hands. I saw her shoulders quiver. A suspicion nibbled at the fringe of my mind, rejected instantly with a spasm of horror.

"Mom! What is it? Who was he?"

I was shocked by the agony of pain in her eyes.

"Oh, Paul!"

I put my hands quickly on her shoulders and shook her gently. "Tell me," I said. "You've got to tell me."

"I can't!"

I was young but I felt very mature and protective and able to take anything. "You don't have to hide anything from me," I said.

Haltingly, she told me about my father and about the brief days she had known him, the short interval of love on which she had built a lonely life. She pleaded with me to feel no bitterness toward the man who was my father. He had given her all he could—love, tenderness, understanding, even a child. She believed that he had really loved her and she had never blamed him for staying away from her. It was the only thing for him to do. She revealed that he had sent her letters in the first months after he left her. She had written at last to tell him that it was better if she dropped out of his life completely. She had not told him about the child.

When she had finished, I felt only pity and love for this woman who had suffered loneliness for the better part of a lifetime in exchange for a love held only for an instant, who had shielded even her bastard son from the truth that might hurt him, who had lived with her memories and her illusion of a life that was, in its own small way, complete.

Anger and bitterness came later. Shame. A feeling that I had been cheated, tricked into believing that I was normal, that I had had a real father just like everyone else. Hatred of the man for the loyalty he had given to another woman.

18

And at last, when the hot flame of anger had burnt itself out, a lasting sense that I was different, I was an outsider.

That night, when my mother's tears had dried and she finally slept with the exhaustion of someone relieved at last of a terrible burden of secrecy, I lay in darkness with my new sense of isolation and my mind returned to the inexplicable vision which had triggered my mother's confession. I wondered what kind of dream could come when one sat with his eyes open in broad daylight, fully conscious. Yet it must have been a dream. The man of the vision was surely someone I had seen, or a projected image of myself, a man whose appearance had made my mother believe I was describing her lover of long ago. Was Ernest Cameron still alive? What would he do or say if the son he didn't know existed should suddenly appear one day to confront him?

I was never to find out. Less than a month later, investigators, easily backtracking along my mother's trail from Albuquerque to Los Angeles, traced her to our modest trailer court. She had been left half of an estate valued at over thirty thousand dollars by one Dr. Ernest Cameron, recently deceased, professor of physics at the University of Illinois, a widower with two married children who had divided the remaining half of his estate. In his will, rewritten after his legal wife's death, Dr. Cameron had revealed the love he had kept secret for almost twenty years.

He had died of injuries suffered in a traffic accident on June 16, 1982. The day of my vision.

Now, nine years later, remembering that extraordinary circumstance as I sat alone in the small bright office, I thought how easily my mother and I had covered up the fearful evidence of the unknown. Almost by deliberate scheme, it seemed, we had failed to investigate the details of my father's death. There was no escaping the fact that I did appear to have dreamed of his accident, but my mother, who was a religious woman, found satisfaction in the belief that God had worked in one of His strange and unquestionable ways. And I found refuge in a recollection of the vision so blurred and hedged with qualifications that I was finally able to believe in coincidence, in a casual dream which had not really mirrored the reality of death occurring thousands of miles away, but had simply reflected some buried fear of violence of my own in a world in which accidental violence was commonplace. Ernest Cameron's death became important only because it brought my mother and me closer together and because it provided the means with which I was able to go to college.

Was I able now fully to believe in my own clairvoyance? Was the earlier vision a symptom of the extra-sensory powers which I was only now discovering in other ways? I had to believe in it. At the same time I was afraid to.

For in my recent dream of violence, I was the victim.

It was ten o'clock that night when I left the massive Liberal Arts Building and started slowly across the sprawling campus. The night classes were over and many of the lights had already gone out. There was a continuous cough and mutter of cars starting and roaring away. Clusters of students drifted by in heated conversation. Couples loitered in the deep shadows of trees or strolled hand in hand with intimate whisper of word and gurgle of laughter. I felt exhausted.

I wandered toward the modern area of stores and restaurants and bars which bordered the campus. I didn't feel like returning to my empty trailer in the hills. At that moment, I keenly regretted the strange compulsion which had kept me from forming close friendships with my colleagues at the university. Perhaps subconsciously I had been avoiding exposure to disillusion or disappointment, but in so doing I had created for myself a lonely place apart.

My path took me past the Science Building. On the first floor there was one panel of windows glowing with light. Most of the building was dark. I stopped for a minute, thinking of Dr. Jonas Temple, the revered geophysicist who was working behind those windows. They were too high to permit me to see into his offices or his laboratories but I knew he would be there. The old man's capacity for work was legendary. And in the past eighteen months those lighted windows had seemed to symbolize man's growing knowledge of life, not only on earth, but in the limitless space in which we whirled. And specifically, of course, on Mars, for Dr. Temple was the man who had directed the exhaustive program of analysis and study of the dead relics of life brought back from the red planet. Like everyone at the university I had been privileged to enter those offices and to stare in wonder at the rows of curious mineral and fossil formations behind the glass doors of their special cabinets. From these, piece by piece, Dr. Temple and his staff were slowly tracing the pattern of Martian evolution.

This night, however, he was probably more concerned with the preparations for the new Martian flight scheduled to begin sometime this month. What lists would he have drawn of things which should be brought back—to reveal what new secrets of the universe?

Once again the world's magnificent adventure made my own private problem seem petty and insignificant. What did it matter in the fantastic wilderness of space and time, one man's personal quarrel with a mind on the edge of anarchy?

I started across the campus again. While standing still I had allowed the October night's chill to penetrate the thin fabric of my coverall. Now my steps quickened. The Dugout, a popular off-campus coffee shop, was nearby, and the thought of steaming hot coffee made me swing toward it.

I was near the edge of the campus when the voice spoke—abrupt, shockingly strong, so real to my ear that I looked around quickly to see who had spoken.

"Is it safe to communicate?"

No one was near me. What I was hearing was in my own mind, a soundless emanation of thought.

"Yes, but softly. We must not be detected now when the time is so close."

I stood rigid at the rim of the dark campus, my whole body taut and quivering, my mind a clean slate upon which the voices wrote. Two of them. There was an individual quality to the thoughts, an inflection and timber of the mind as unmistakable as the personal tone of a human voice, yet oddly sexless and unemotional. The first one I had heard was more tentative in his vibrations, less in control of his power, giving the impression that he was younger; the second was older, heavier, more authoritative in his strength.

"You are comfortable?" the second voice asked.

"Yes."

"The new body is healthy?"

"Completely."

I began to move, sensing in a way I couldn't comprehend the direction from which the thoughts were coming. I stumbled along the side street which led to the Dugout, tracking the bodiless pulsations as an animal trails a scent.

The older one spoke again. "You had no difficulty with the parents?"

"They suspected nothing."

The voices were closer now, but I was alone on the street except for a couple ambling along the shadowed sidewalk a block away. And why would they have to communicate with their minds when they walked arm in arm? I didn't question the actual existence of the voices in my mind. At that moment I believed in them as naturally and unquestioningly as I accepted vocal speech. They were there. I heard them. Even the meaningless question about a "new body" did not make me wonder if the voices were hallucinatory. To talk of bodies as if they could be shed like garments and new ones tried for fit and comfort was nonsense, but I had no thought of making sense of the words I had heard. I wanted only to find their source.

And suddenly I was standing in front of the Dugout

staring through the steam-clouded windows. The place was almost empty.

"What is it that you wish me to do?" The young one, calm, matter-of-fact in its subservience. It? He or she? I had no way of telling.

"You have a job—an important one."

There was no doubting the fact that they were inside the Dugout. The sense of mental presence was overpowering, as if one were in a corner of a dark closet listening to two strangers who had huddled in the tiny space and closed the door to whisper confidentially.

"Have you heard—"

I opened the door. Four students in a booth against the wall turned to stare at me. There was a sudden, total silence.

Instinct made me walk casually to the counter, where I slipped onto a stool so placed that I would be able to see the booths along the right wall without deliberately or obviously turning my head. Lois, the waitress who was on night duty at the Dugout, sauntered toward me along the narrow aisle behind the counter.

"What'll you have, Mr. Cameron?"

"Coffee, Lois."

"Coming right up!"

It never occurred to me to consider Lois as a possible agent of the thoughts I had heard. She was a student who had been working a part-time evening shift in the Dugout for almost two full semesters. She was more notable for the ripeness of breast and hip than for any indication of unusual mental capacities. I was surprised that she was still in school and not already married to one of the students who were always flirting with her across the counter. Her blonde, buxom beauty and open friendliness went better with children and home cooking than books and short order food.

The place was unusually quiet. At first I saw no one but Lois and the four students together in a front booth. Two of them I had recognized—Mike Boyle, who had been an All-Coast tackle the previous season and might make All-American this year, and Laurie Hendricks, a disturbing redhead who sat in the front row of my eleven o'clock sophomore English class. The other boy's blond crewcut and immature good looks seemed faintly familiar probably because they were typical of so many students. The second girl, who sat next to Mike Boyle, was small and pretty and brunette. I had never seen her before.

All four looked much too normal, as they returned to their animated talk, to be part of the weird experience which had brought me there. They had given me only a casual glance. They seemed to be genuinely ignoring me as I sipped my coffee, trying to study the group without seeming to.

The next thought came without warning from the back of the room. "Have you heard anything else of the listener?"

I swallowed a deep hot draught of coffee, scalding my throat. Bending low over the counter, I struggled to keep from choking and coughing. The cup rattled in the saucer as I set it down.

I knew that I was the listener.

"Whispers. Nothing I could be sure of."

The question had come from the back, the answer was closer. I was convinced that the reply came from one of the four students in the booth not more than fifteen feet away from me.

Then I saw a hand move at the table of the last booth near the rear of the restaurant. A man's hand stirring coffee absently. He sat with his back toward me, concealed behind the high back of the booth. His was the older, heavier mental voice.

"He must be found," the man's thought came.

"Could it be—a foreign intruder? Perhaps even one of us who—"

"No. Soon we will be many—when I come back. But now we are the only ones. He must be human."

"But he speaks with the mind."

24

"That is not so strange. It is only strange that many do not do so, as we do."

Listening, I felt a creeping contraction of horror as if I had touched something cold and alien. My God, what did they mean? They believed that I must be—human. And what were they?

"I would like to return with you—to assist in your expedition." The bright young mind spoke.

"Your task is to find the human who speaks with his thoughts and destroy him. If he is able to hear us he is dangerous. Once we are here in force it will not matter. But now——"

The horror expanded in my mind, a revulsion exaggerated now by a consciousness of danger, of menace that was suddenly close and real. While they were hunting me, the listener, I had stumbled right into their midst. Who they were or what I did not know, but they held power in their minds beyond the scope of my imagination. And if they learned that I was—

"When do you go?" the youthful one asked.

"Soon now. The launching will be in the final week of this month, depending on suitable conditions."

"You will be able to effect the transfer?"

"There will be no difficulty in the actual change. I have already picked out the human in the space colony. He is young and strong but mentally very susceptible. Already he is under my control. I have only to find the right moment alone with him. However, since this body I now inhabit must be presumed dead when I leave it, and there will be no visible remains, it will be necessary for me to devise an accident in which the body would naturally be consumed or lost. Drowning may prove most suitable."

Drowning! My recurrent nightmare came back to me in a rush. I felt the blood drain from my face. My head felt light and faintly dizzy.

"I do not fully understand about the body," the young one thought.

"It is a superb instrument," the other replied, "but

25

unfortunately not as dense in its material structure as those we are accustomed to inhabit. You will find that your energies will draw excessively on the body's matter. You must take great care to maintain constant control over the body shell to keep it from disintegrating too rapidly. At the same time the vital organs must not be damaged. In time, perhaps, these human bodies may adapt to our needs more satisfactorily. Until then periodic changes will be needed. I have conserved my present form only because it was vital to our plans."

"When will you make the exchange?"

"At the last possible moment—when close physical examination is no longer likely and when it is too late for the launching to be delayed."

"You might require my services when you have to take over the ship—"

"No! It is vital that you remain behind. You must understand that I might not return. Anything could happen in space. If I should fail to come back, it is still possible that others of us will be brought to earth on other ships. If the humans are more careful than before, our brothers might never escape.

It will be up to you effect their release."

"Yes, that is clear."

Suddenly I put my hands over my ears, pressing my palms hard against my skull as if the barrier of bone and tissue might cut off the bewildering voices that stole into my brain. This was not real, not possible! This was madness. Not aliens from outer space, plotting to take over the space ships and use them to bring back hordes of aliens. Not beings who could possess and use human bodies. I couldn't believe in these.

"Mr. Cameron?"

"What?" I looked up, startled and frightened, into the wondering blue eyes of the blonde waitress.

"More coffee?"

"Oh. Yes. Yes, please."

My voice cracked. The hand that spooned sugar into the

26

cup shook. My body was seized by momentary spasms. Fear. Fear that demoralized body and mind.

Then I realized that the strange voices were silent. But there was a suspenseful quality to the silence, an indefinable tension of waiting. Had I done something to betray myself? Had the lash of fear been audible?

Slowly my gaze swung toward the booth in the back of the room. The man had withdrawn further out of sight. Even his hand was no longer visible. I forced myself to glance at the booth where the students were still talking, low-voiced, the steady murmur split by wedges of laughter. Laurie Hendricks' eyes met mine in a brief instant of recognition. She was smiling and her green eyes were speculative. At that moment, the blond youth spoke to her and she turned toward him, red mouth opening in laughter.

I looked away. Several yards down the counter Lois was busily wiping an imaginary spot on the gleaming surface. I lit a cigarette with a painstaking effort at steadiness and sat staring at the curl of steam rising from the coffee to blend with the denser cloud of cigarette smoke.

And something probed at my brain. My reaction was instinctive, like a turtle withdrawing under its shell with surprising speed. I froze my mind, shutting off all thought. I was nothing. I was blankness. I was neither thought nor emotion nor awareness. The eerie mental sensation came again, like a child's stick prodding the turtle's shell to see if it would move or to find a soft, vulnerable spot in the protective casing A thought probing at my brain, trying to force an entry, but there was no opening.

The tentative pressure ceased. For a moment there was silence except for the murmuring at the nearby booth and the clatter of dishes as Lois piled them into a steel sink. Slowly I allowed awareness to return.

"All right." The older one was communicating again.

"What happened?"

"I was not certain. For a moment I thought——" The message broke off. "I must leave."

"When shall we speak again?"

27

"We must avoid all contact unless absolutely necessary. There is too much risk of detection. We should never be together again in the same place until the listener is found."

"What shall I do when I find him?"

There was a brief pause. I found myself tense as I waited for the reply, my hands clenching painfully.

"It must look like an accident."

Laughter erupted from the booth nearby, raucous and free, the young gay laughter of a normal, healthy world. I had the sudden, bitter feeling that I had left this world forever and its laughter was rude and jarring on my nerves, a bizarre punctuation to the sentence of death I had just heard pronounced on myself.

Then the students were pushing out of their booth, moving toward the door, passing near me.

"Hi, Mr. Cameron!" Laurie Hendricks called.

I nodded. My throat was constricted, unable to open for speech. The group spilled out onto the sidewalk and I felt a stab of alarm. One of them was an alien—but what could I do? How could I find out which one? Should I follow them or the man in the booth?

I shot a glance toward the rear booth. I caught a fleeting glimpse of a dark gray suit as the man disappeared down the narrow corridor which led to the restrooms.

And to a rear exit.

I stumbled to my feet, throwing a coin onto the counter. For a second I was caught in the dilemma of divided choice. Then I strode decisively through the restaurant toward the back hall. When I reached it it was empty. I whirled and raced to the front door.

The four students were across the street strolling onto the campus grounds. I trotted after them. They seemed oblivious of me. I could see the small dark-haired girl clinging to Mike Boyle's arm. The blond boy spoke confidentially in Laurie Hendick's ear. I stopped on the far side of the street, hesitating, watching them walk slowly across the green lawn. I couldn't follow them closely without being seen. I would have to keep at a distance.

I glanced back toward the Dugout. A man stood on the sidewalk to the left of the restaurant in the shadow of a store front. Even though I couldn't see his face I could feel the impact of his eyes. He had not been there when I came out of the Dugout. My scalp prickled. I started at the shadowy figure. For a moment neither of us moved.

What I did then was incredibly foolish, and yet it was not a consciously deliberate act, not even a careless impulse. Rather I spoke to myself, voicing the question that filled my mind but unconsicously projecting it toward the unknown man who watched me across the street.

"Who are you?"

Afterwards I could not be sure what happened, but in that split second as the thought was directed toward the dark figure I seemed to catch a quick reaction of startled surprise. I was immediately shocked by my own stupidity. I had betrayed myself. Now they knew who I was.

And at that moment I saw the headlights of a car speeding toward me along the near side of the street, its lights bouncing as the car rode over a bump. Something held me there on the sidewalk close to the curb as the car approached swiftly. And suddenly it was very close, the eyes of its headlights holding my gaze hypnotized, the hum of its engine swelling in my ears.

"Now! Into the street!"

The command struck my mind with the force of a blow. I tottered forward, tripping clumsily over the curb. I had an awareness of struggling feebly, of trying to control rubbery limbs with a mind that was weak and confused, of flailing my arms wildly at the air.

"In front of the car! Fall!"

And I flung myself forward into the blinding glare of the onrushing headlights. There was a tearing screech of brakes, a scream that seemed far away, and a massive blur of metal brushing by me as I fell.

4

I SEEM TO be swimming up through thick layers of black asphalt. There were voices, angry and frightened, but they would never find me down here under the surface.

"It wasn't my fault, dammit! He jumped right in front of me."

"You were going too fast."

"I tell you he was trying to kill himself! It wasn't my fault!"

"You're lucky he wasn't killed."

I opened my eyes. A ring of faces stared down at me. Eyes and mouths round and big and open. For a moment I gazed at them numbly without feeling or thought. The numbness began to fade and I felt the tickling sensation of returning fear. All of the faces showed concern or anixety. One was the face of a stranger. The driver of the car, I thought. And one of the faces was a mask behind which hid a thing incomprehensible and terrible.

"Mr. Cameron! Are you all right?"

I looked into the large green eyes of Laurie Hendricks. They were remarkably beautiful eyes, framed by thick dark lashes, their color deep and vivid. Now they were very wide and troubled. The smooth plane of her forehead was faintly creased with worry and her lips were parted over even white teeth. She was someone I had never really seen before. I had been abstractedly aware of red hair and a pair of slim calves crossed and a figure that strained a sweater—but I had never clearly seen the person.

Was she the one?

"You okay, professor?"

My eyes shifted to Mike Boyle and I had a quick impression of his massive, powerful body towering over me.

"Yes, I—I think so."

I stared at each of them—Laurie, Boyle, the blond youth, the little brunette with small, demure features, the red-faced stranger who appeared to be more angry than concerned. The memory of the car's fender brushing past me as I fell returned so vividly that a reaction hit me. I had to fight down the impulse to get away, to run, to limp, to hobble, even to crawl, just so that I could be away from the thing that watched me, luring behind anxious human eyes.

"What the hell did you do that for?" It was the stranger speaking, the driver of the car.

"I—I tripped."

"Jesus Christ, you could have got killed!"

"Yes. I'm sorry."

I sat up. Hands reached down to help me and I flinched at their touch. I moved my legs and felt along my arms and ribs. Nothing seemed to be broken. There were no sharp pains, only a mass of aches blending into one. I had been very lucky. The next time they would make sure that I wouldn't escape.

Mike Boyle put a meaty hand under my arm and lifted me to my feet with the casual ease of an adult hoisting a child in the air. Could all that muscle hide a super brain?

I steeled myself to peer across the street at the spot where the man had stood watching me. The sidewalk was empty.

"You been drinking, Mr. Cameron?" the blond boy asked with a grin.

I smiled stiffly. "Coffee. I can't explain what happened. I just lost my balance and fell. It was almost as if someone had pushed me."

I watched the boy's eyes closely but they betrayed no reaction.

"Well, I can't stand around here all night," the red-faced man said belligerently, making the statement a challenge. "I guess you're not hurt."

"No. I don't think so. The car just missed me."

"Maybe you better get his name, Mr. Cameron," the blond youth suggested.

31

"Yeah, you might have internal injuries or something," Mike Boyle put in.

"What the hell does he need my name for?"

I suddenly wondered if I should so quickly dismiss the stranger from suspicion. Hadn't his car appeared rather fortuitously? And hadn't he been racing too fast?

"Yes, I'd better have your name," I said.

"Now, wait a minute, if you think you're going to sue me—"

"I have no intention of sueing, but I'd better have your name. You do have insurance, I suppose?"

"Yeah, but—"

"Do you want me to get a cop, Mr. Cameron," the blond boy asked aggressively.

I looked at the red-faced stranger. "I don't think that will be necessary."

The suggestion of bringing the police into the affair convinced the man. He fished out his driver's license. Laurie Hendricks found a pencil in her purse and wrote out the name and address. Albert Harrison, Trailer G12, 444 San Rafael Road. I got the name of his insurance company and told him that was all I needed. Then he insisted on having my name and address. I hesitated, glancing at the four listening students. Then I realized that it didn't matter. They could easily find out where I lived through the school. I was even conveniently listed in the telephone directory.

Harrison finally marched off in a bad temper, obviously afraid that I would discover some non-existent injuries the following day. I was reasonably convinced that he was innocent, but it was just as well to know his name. And to know where to find him.

"Are you sure you're feeling all right, Mr. Cameron?"

Laurie Hendricks had moved close to me. As she spoke she rested a hand lightly on my arm and raised those incredible green eyes to meet mine. I felt the bold collison of our stares. Her figures burned through the sleeve of my jacket, and I caught the subtle drift of the flower fragrance she wore.

"Yes," I said slowly. "Thanks for helping."

"We could drive you home," Mike Boyle offered without enthusiasm. "I've got my car."

"That won't be necessary."

And suddenly I looked at the slender girl standing beside Boyle, realizing that she was the only one of the group who had not said a word. She was watching me with curious interest. Catching my gaze she smiled.

"Yes, we'd be glad to drive you. Mike wouldn't mind."

She looked up at the big football player and slipped her hand under his arm with a slight suggestion of possessiveness. Ordinarily the gesture would have made me smile. Even now it caused my quick suspicion to evaporate.

And I realized that I couldn't really believe that any of these four normal young people could be anything but what they seemed. To think otherwise was absurd—and yet I had heard one of them instructed to kill me.

Or had I?

And all of the tormenting doubt and fear of the past months returned. Could I have imagined everything—the voices, the attempt to kill me, the mysterious beings from outer space? Was all that an elaborate concoction of a diseased mind?

There was nothing imaginary about the fall in front of the speeding car. But what if there were no enemies except those in my own mind? The meaning of this possibility was harrowingly clear. For then I had tried to kill myself.

I saw the blond boy's feet shifting in evident impatience. I surveyed the group once more and my eyes lingered on Laurie Hendricks' upturned face, on the soft shimmer of her bright red hair.

"You kids go on," I said. "I'm all right now."

I turned and walked away, not looking back.

5

IT WAS A bright morning. Through the high windows of the classroom came soft sunlight filtered through the delicate fiberglass grillwork that faced the entire west side of the building. I looked down at the peaceful campus, the slowly moving streams of students, the expanse of cool green grass, the solid impressiveness of nearby buildings. In the distance I could see a section of the practice football field and I thought of Mike Boyle, driving his huge shoulder into a tackling dummy, sweating and grunting, thick thighs driving powerfully. A monstrous youth, all right. But an unearthly monster? Hardly.

I heard the restless movement in the room behind me and I wrenched my thoughts back to the lecture.

"Why is *Beowulf* called an epic?" I asked rhetorically, turning. "Because of its scope. Because of the greatness of its hero. Because it expresses the whole struggle and aspiration and point of view of its people. Its action is on a grand scale. Its emotions are deep and powerful. This is not the twentieth century story of a housewife who has a petty little affair with a mediocre man she meets in the super market. This is big. This is important. It has to do with the vital issues of life. It has greatness. Victory is a triumph over a formidable enemy of the people. Defeat is death, and even in the manner of dying there is majesty and heroism." I paused, letting my eyes rove over the room, using the teacher's trick of focusing on the last row and thus seeming to be looking at all of the students in between. Their faces were all turned toward me in a semblance of respectful attention. A boy in the third row was sleeping with his eyes half open. "And the manner of the writing is in keeping with the heroic action," I went on, letting my gaze move forward to the front row, to the shock of flaming red hair

34

and a pair of carelessly crossed legs sleekly clad in spun plastisheen. "It is powerful, strongly rhythmic, eloquent."

I smiled. Laurie Hendricks seemed to sigh, and the slight movement brought my attention to her breasts, softly outlined under a lemon-colored sweater.

"Of course it loses much in translation," I added. There was a respectful titter of amusement from the class. The old prof, I thought, with his academic jokes. Even at twenty-seven, in my fourth year of teaching, I had fallen into the habit of repeating the same jokes each semester. Laurie Hendricks smiled warmly at me and I found myself reacting to the moist red curve of her lips, liking the fact that she had been amused.

During the long, relatively sleepless night, my faith in the validity of my mind's impressions had wavered badly. I had ranged from an angry conviction that everything I had heard was real and true, through all the stages of argument and doubt, down to a dismal hopelessness, an acknowledgment that alien minds and macabre plots were grotesque splinters off my peculiar branch of insanity.

Looking now at Laurie Hendricks, I found myself reluctant to believe that she was anything but an unusually beautiful girl who was giving every indication of being more than ordinarily interested in me. The accidental circumstance of the previous night's meeting had created a new relationship between us without a word being spoken this morning. She was no longer just another anonymous student. And I strongly suspected that I was no longer to her just another stuffy instructor.

I turned abruptly toward the sleeping boy in the third row. "Mr. Carbo," I said sharply. "Mr. Carbo!"

His head came up with a snap. His eyes were still dull with sleep. "Huh?"

"Mr. Carbo, are you with us?"

The class laughed, warming to a situation in which some-else is made to look a little ridiculous.

"Mr. Carbo, what do you think of Beowulf's technique in handling the dragon?"

"I don't think I understand, sir," the boy said lamely.

"You have read the assignment I suppose."

"Yes, sir."

"Did anything strike you about the fight?"

"Well, I thought it was kind of bloodthirsty, sir."

"The Anglo-Saxons were a bloodthirsty people," I said. "They didn't have television or movies or synthetic-participation sports to let them drain off some of their violence. Even their literature was more like a battle cry than a civilized catharsis of emotions."

"Yes, sir."

"I'm glad you agree, Mr. Carbo." I felt that I was being rather hard on him, but you were expected to make a goat out of the guilty student who slept or talked or failed to study. It was standard teaching procedure and not without its value in keeping the class on its toes.

I let him off the hook, turning to address the class as a whole. "You know how boxers will waste the first round feeling each other out, testing the other's reactions? Did you notice anything similar in Beowulf's approach to battle?"

"Yeah," a student called from the back of the room. "He lets the dragon gobble up a couple of the other guys."

"Right!" I said with exaggerated enthusiasm. "Miss Hendricks, would you read that passage for us?"

She looked startled. As she hunted for the place there was a general thud and rustle of textbooks being hastily opened. Laurie Hendricks coughed and began to read. Her voice was low, hesitant, pleasantly husky. The passage she read told in gory detail how the ancient hero had watched as the dragon entered the mead hall, had waited, feigning sleep, studying the enemy's movements, even though this involved a rather grim death for some of Beowulf's companions in arms. As I listened, I thought of the younger alien the night before, standing among the students on the campus and watching while the other flung me into the street in front of the racing car. I heard the words of the centuries-old epic and a detached portion of my mind told me that, unlike the mighty Anglo-Saxon warrior, I couldn't wait out the enemy. I already knew how he worked. If I waited there would be another accident. I had to find the enemy before he or she had a chance to attack.

Laurie Hendricks finished reading and glanced up questioningly from the text. I nodded to indicate that that was enough. My gaze held hers.

"The point I'm making," I said, "is that the attitude toward life was so different from ours. Unless you understand and accept that difference you can't respond to the literature of the people at that time. Their view of the universe was alien to anything we know. Human life was cheap. To stay alive was a constant struggle. Life didn't last very long—"

The bell rang to signal the end of the lecture. I held up my hand, stilling the immediate mass movement out of the seats.

"I have to talk to you individually about your term papers," I said quickly, ignoring the general groan. "I'll set up individual appointments. If the students in the—first row—will stay a few minutes I'll start with them."

I nodded and the class burst into a confusion of noise and movement. The students in the first row lingered. I sat behind the desk in the front of the room and waved the initial student forward. Carefully I drew up a time schedule of office appointments. As I had hoped, Laurie Hendricks waited until the last. We were alone in the classroom when she uncurled from her seat and swayed toward the desk. The soft curve of her mouth was provocative.

"You don't look any the worse for wear, Professor."

I smiled faintly. "I'm only an instructor, Miss Hendricks, not a professor. And I feel fine, thanks to you and your friends."

"We just picked you up and dusted you off."

There was a brief, awkward silence. Our eyes met appraisingly. She leaned a firmly rounded hip against the edge of the desk.

"I'd like to thank your friends personally," I said at last. "Would you give me their names?"

"Sure—but you don't have to thank them."

"I'd like to. I know Mike Boyle, of course—but who was the girl with him?"

"That's Helen Darrow. She's a physics major. She and Mike are going steady now."

I looked surprised. The girl hadn't seemed like the kind who would be majoring in physics. And that fact didn't go along with a co-ed's worshipful admiration of a brawny football star.

"They're a funny couple," Laurie Hendricks said, patting her red heir with graceful fingers. "But sometimes a man and a woman can clink together when you'd least expect it."

I smiled. "And who was your boy friend?"

"My boy fr--oh, you mean Bob. That's Bob Jenkins. But we're just friends, Professor."

I wished that she would ease off a little on the steam she was generating. Her invitation was too open, too sudden. I felt a tickling wariness inside as I looked into the green eyes.

"Did you have something in mind for me, Professor?" she asked, her voice almost purring. "I mean, about the term paper."

"Yes. Suppose we set up a time. . ." I stared at the schedule I had started to draw up. A half-formed plan jumped into focus in my mind and I knew that subconsciously I had known all along what I hoped to arrange. I spoke impulsively. "How about tonight, Miss Hendricks?"

"Tonight?" Her face showed surprise, but I saw the flicker of something else momentarily in her eyes. Satisfaction.

"My time is pretty well taken up for the next two days during the day—with classes and these other appointments. But I do have some free time tonight."

"In your office?"

I hesitated. "You could come up to my trailer. I'm at the

top of the hills near Beverly Glen. The Valley View Trailer Court. It's quite easy to reach."

"I know the place. Off Mulholland, isn't it?"

"Yes. I'm in number 14-P."

She was smiling broadly now. "That sounds fine to me—Mr. Cameron."

"About eight?"

"I'll be there."

She eased away from the desk and started across the room. I found myself watching the rhythmic motion of her hips. At the door she turned to give me a parting invitation over her shoulder.

I didn't move. Through the door I saw the young blond boy, Jenkins, join her in the corridor. He grinned and took her hand in a casually intimate way. I felt a tug of—

My God! I thought. Jealousy. Envy.

And I wondered what was my real motive for asking her to come to my trailer that evening. Feeling out the enemy? Narrowing down my list of suspects? But if there were any possibility that she could be possessed by a powerful alien being it would be incredibly dangerous to be alone with her.

I wouldn't have a chance.

The point was that I didn't want to believe that she was the enemy—and I did want to be alone with her.

6

JACK HESS, ANOTHER of the younger instructors in the English department, asked me if I'd like to go to a nearby drive-in for lunch. I hesitated—and suddenly remembered Lois, the blonde waitress in the Dugout. Once again I had been stupid!

"No—not today, Jack," I said quickly. "I've got something on."

He looked at me quizzically, shrugged and turned away. I knew most of my colleagues thought me an odd one, reserved and even anti-social. Jack had made more of an effort than the others to be friendly. I was quite aware that my feeling of being an outsider was an unhealthy one but I couldn't help it.

I left hurriedly and strode hastily across the campus. How could I have overlooked such an obvious factor? Lois was sure to have seen the man in the back booth the night before. At the least she would have brought him his coffee. Even if he was a stranger to her, she would be able to describe him to me. And perhaps he wasn't a stranger. Maybe he came in often.

The little restaurant was jammed with students. I pushed my way to the end of the counter. Lois wasn't in sight. I waited until Harry, the sweating, somewhat greasy-faced owner of the Dugout, came near me.

"Can I talk to you a minute, Harry?"

He glanced at me, recognized me as a steady customer, and probably shrewdly placed me for what I was, a not very important young teacher.

"Can't it wait? I'm busy as hell."

He hurried back up the aisle without waiting for an answer. Harry did some of the cooking, but during the rush hours he helped out on tables or behind the counter while the regular cook took care of the orders.

In a moment he was back, flopping open an order pad. "What'll it be?"

"Hamburger and coffee," I said. "Where's Lois?"

His eyes went flat and cold. "She doesn't come on until later. Why?"

"I wanted to talk to her. What time does she get here?"

"Look, Jack, the girl has enough trouble with the kids around here without—"

"I only want to talk to her."

"Yeah." His manner was openly belligerent. "I'll turn in your order."

He spun away. It was several minutes before I could

catch him again. I was aware that some students nearby were staring at me, but I didn't care.

When Harry did come within earshot, I spoke quickly. "Harry, I was in an accident outside your place last night. Right in front. I think Lois might have seen it and I want to ask her a few questions. Now how about it? What time does she come on duty?"

He looked mollified though his manner was still brusque. "Six o'clock," he grunted. "She's on from six to midnight."

I frowned. Now that the possibility of her identifying the stranger in the back booth had occurred to me, I was nervous and impatient to talk to her. Six o'clock was a long way away. A lot of things could happen before six.

When my order finally came I leaned forward and spoke urgently to Harry. "I'd like to reach her as soon as possible," I said. "Do you have her phone number?"

The aggressive coldness hardened his face instantly. His eyes were small and their expression bleak.

"I don't set up dates with the help," he said. "Even for teachers. That'll be two dollars and a quarter," he added pointedly, jerking his head toward the thin sandwich and coffee.

Irritated, I threw the money onto the counter. I would get no more information out of him. I realized that his suspicion was too quickly aroused to be normal. The chances were that he wanted Lois himself, probably didn't get anywhere with her in the face of the competition, and the constant spectacle of men and boys flirting with her in his restaurant kept him on the raw edge of frustrated anger.

Impatience gnawed at me, but there was nothing I could do but wait. I stood hesitating outside the restaurant, wondering if I should go to the registrar's office to try to find out where Lois lived. I might run into trouble. I was already planing to break one of the academic rules by arranging to have Laurie Hendricks visit my trailer that evening, but at least I had a plausible reason—and in spite of the rules, meetings with students in the home over class projects were not unusual. For me to try to get the address

41

or phone number of a young and obviously endowed co-ed who was not in any of my classes was something else again.

I spent the afternoon, except for one lecture at two o'clock, in the safety of the library stacks. I complied a bibliography of recent publications in the library on the subject of life on other planets. There was a special section of articles and research projects concerning Mars, most of them written by Dr. Temple himself or members of his staff. It would take much more than one afternoon to burrow through all the material, and I might not have many afternoons.

I had to act on the premise that I was sane, that I had overheard aliens conferring telephathically, that the conviction they were determined to destroy me was not a delusion. They were real. They menaced not only my safety but that of the world. And they planned to bring others of their kind back to Earth. These were the facts I had to begin with.

They pointed directly to Mars.

I was surprised at the unaimity of scientific opinion concerning the possibility of life on other planets. In our solar system, there was only one planet other than Earth which could possibly support life as we understood it. On the other planets either heat or the lack of it, the presence of poisonous gases or the absence of atmosphere, argued that life could not exist. There might well be planets in other solar systems with conditions conducive to the existence of an intelligent life form, but in ours there was only Earth—and the planet man had reached in his first great conquest of space: Mars.

There had long been heated scientific debate on the possibility of Mars supporting life, especially after the discovery of the famous canals. Even observations from the moon during the late 1970's and the 1980's had not settled the issue or resolved the mystery of the canals. There had always been a dedicated group who maintained that life on the red planet was not only possible but probable.

Then came the successful mission in 1989-90. I didn't

have to read the innumerable articles to know the general facts about what humans had found there—and what they had failed to find. There was life in the form of vegetation and microscopic organisms. There was even animal life— a tiny reptile which had been seen and photographed but had shown such remarkable elusiveness that it had never been trapped alive. Besides these, there were clear signs of a dead civilization that had been created by intelligent beings. Crude by our standards, especially in crafts and tools, but intelligent. These discoveries served only to create the new Martian mystery. The planet abounded in fossil remains of lower animals. Nothing else. Nothing that seemed capable of the intelligence which had wrought the civilization of Mars and dug its amazing network of canals. It was as if the intelligent beings which had ruled the planets thousands of years ago had simply left it. They had not died there. Or they had mysteriously dissolved, leaving no trace of themselves except their handiwork, leaving behind a dying planet.

Mars was the only place from which the aliens could have come, I thought—but no intelligent aliens had returned on the space ship. Even the specimens of plant life had failed to survive the trip back to earth. And yet—

I tried to remember exactly what I had overhead. The voices had talked of a launching soon. And the fact was that a new flight to Mars was scheduled to take place. They had talked of it as returning to their own place of origin, to their fellows. But if they needed a space ship in which to return, they must have come on our ship.

And nothing had come. I read, in the dusty silence of the library's inner stacks, the accounts of what had happened when the one great ship came home to Earth. All of the survivors had been exhaustively investigated through complex physical and mental tests. No alien presence could have escaped that examination. Weren't they afraid even now of detection? Wasn't that why they wanted my own death to be accidental? Even every fragment of rock and bone and dried-up fungus had been painstakingly tested not once but over and over again. No alien life had come. I was trying to believe the impossible.

With each page turned during that long afternoon my depression grew. When at last, my eyes hot and raw with strain, I set aside the material I had read, a pitifully small portion of the total on my list, I had found not one single hopeful fact. But hope persisted. Perhaps there was something I had overlooked, or something in the later investigations I had not yet had time to read, that would offer a clue. And there was Lois—

I looked at my watch. It was a few minutes after six. Hastily I sorted the material I had read from the rest. The former I returned to the librarian, leaving the unread papers and magazines on the small desk which I had reserved in the stacks. I ran across the cool green of the campus. When I reached the street near the Dugout, I hung back from the sidewalk, waiting until there were no moving cars in sight. It would be all too easy for them to use the same technique a second time.

At this hour of the evening, the Dugout was not crowded. There were students in a few of the booths and at the counter. I recognized a history professor and a zoologist talking quietly at one end of the counter. Lois was not there. Another girl was working the tables, the same girl who had been on duty earlier in the day, and Harry himself was still behind the counter. He glared at me as I approached.

"Where is Lois?" I asked anxiously.

"How the hell should I know? Maybe you can tell me."

"She hasn't come in?"

"No, she hasn't come in." Harry obviously blamed me.

"Look, Harry, I told you I just wanted to ask her a couple of questions: It's important. But that's all I want." I paused. "Didn't she call or anything?"

"No," he grunted, less nastily. "Sometimes she's late. Sometimes she doesn't come in at all."

I felt a hollowness in my stomach. She had to come. I had to talk to her.

I sat at the counter and ordered coffee. I waited. The two teachers farther down the counter nodded at me. Students left and a few more trickled in. Every time the door opened I looked up eagerly. I ordered more coffee and let it grow cold in front of me, untouched.

An hour passed. Harry paused in front of me. He spoke grudgingly, apparently convinced at last that I was not lying. "You gonna eat? I don't think she's coming tonight."

"No, I'm not hungry. Has she ever done this before—just stayed away without telling you?"

"Yeah, sometimes." His face clouded. "These kids—"

I thought of my date with Laurie Hendricks. Lois might show up later. She had probably gone out with some student. Apparently she could be careless about her hours. Harry wasn't going to fire her no matter what she did. Yes, she would probably be in later. I could come back after Laurie left.

At seven-thirty I gave up. I just had time to get back to my trailer court before eight. It took me five minutes to walk to the local elevated station. There was another five minutes wait before a car slid swiftly out of the gathering darkness. Moments later I alighted at the Mulholland platform where the local connected with the Mulholland elevated.

I walked back to the trailer.

It was dark when I let myself in. My neighbor, the strangely withdrawn girl with the surprising figure, sat eating in her brightly lit room, the blinds partly open at the front of her trailer. Another lonely one, I thought. Another outsider.

But tonight I wouldn't be alone.

7

By EIGHT-THIRTY that evening, I was becoming uneasy. I had had an evening full of impatient waiting and the strain was telling on my nerves. I was beginning to feel like a man with a cold or some other rare disease, shunned and avoided. I kept rising and going to the windows to peer out, expecting each time to see Laurie Hendricks just turning up the walk. Each time I was disappointed.

I don't know what I had actually expected to happen when she came. I had told myself that the reason for asking her was clear: she was suspect. Even if I didn't think she was guilty I had to make sure, and the opportunity to meet her privately had been easy to create. But there was another reason. My self-imposed isolation had had a number of drawbacks. When I thought of the clean limbs I had seen so often displayed in the front row of that eleven o'clock English class, when I remembered the way her sweaters were pulled taut across her chest, I felt a different shakiness that made my throat dry and my palms moist.

The wall clock kept changing numbers, approaching nine, and still she didn't arrive. I began to question the eagerness with which she had accepted the suggestion of meeting me at my trailer. Had it all been an act to lull any suspicions I might have? Set him up for it. Make him jumpy. Dull his mind with a little sex play. Then arrange a convenient accident. Easy. He's ripe for it. He hadn't had a woman in over two years. He won't be thinking of anything else. He'll never believe that a young, beautiful girl could be a—

The rap on the door was so light that for a moment I wasn't sure I had actually heard a sound. Then it came again, a gentle rapping, clearly audible. I stared at the door and all of a sudden my palms were clammy again, and I didn't know if the reaction was from desire or fear.

She was standing on the step just outside the door, looking up. When I didn't say anything, she smiled apologetically, the curve of her lips tentative and strongly appealing.

"I'm sorry I'm late, Mr. Cameron. I was—held up."

"Come in," I said stiffly. "It doesn't matter."

She stepped up into the small living room. The moment she entered the room it seemed to shrink, filled with the physical fact of her presence. I closed the door, feeling self-conscious about the action as if it were overtly aggressive. I stared at her. She wore one of the popular one-piece coveralls knitted of a chemical fiber in a red-and-white diamond pattern. The clinging suit was not exactly the usual costume for a student visiting her instructor.

She glanced curiously around the room. "This is nice," she said.

"It's not exactly spacious but I get by. And the view is good."

I indicated the glittering panorama visible through the window in the end wall. She moved closer to it and looked out into the night. I suddenly wondered if someone else was outside waiting for her signal. The other alien. I made a conscious effort of concentration, listening with my mind. I seemed to have a strange sensation of hearing the world's slow murmur like the distant sounds of traffic on a road far, far below you. But nothing else.

Something made me glance out the side window. I was just in time to see the face of the girl next door, set and unsmiling, before her blinds snapped shut. I closed my own draperies, feeling the tension easing in me. So my neighbor wasn't above doing a little window watching of her own, I thought, half-smiling.

"I meant to be here on time," Laurie said, still staring out the window. "But Bob dropped in and—and sometimes he's difficult."

"Jenkins?"

"Yes. We were supposed to have a date tonight."

I looked at the line of the zipper that traced the curving

47

column of her spine, realizing how easily the clinging suit could be shed and acutely aware that she wore nothing underneath it.

"I don't blame him," I said. "I'd be jealous, too."

She pivoted slowly, pleasure glowing in her striking green eyes. And I realized how young she really was. Twenty at most, I thought. Her skin was flawlessly smooth, clear and unlined. Her every movement had the supple grace and vitality of youth. Yet she was a woman, already wise in the way of women.

I caught myself. What did I really know of her? How could I know the mind which controlled this youthful animal beauty? And I thought of a cunning super-intelligence watching me from behind the cool green of her eyes, amused, toying with me. Or did they have a sense of humor? I had caught nothing humorous in the words I had overheard. I had sensed something infinitely cold, completely emotionless.

"Daddy says I'm spoiled," Laurie Hendricks said abruptly.

"Daddy?" I repeated stupidly.

"Yes. I do have one, you know." She shrugged and the gesture caused a wonderful interplay of movement under the tight coverall. "But he's the one who spoiled me, so he shouldn't complain. He thinks I just amuse myself with men and he doesn't like it."

"Do you?"

She laughed, the warm rippling sound making my skin tingle like an electric current. "Of course," she said. "Why shouldn't I?"

"I suspect you're rich," I said. "It's funny, I hadn't thought of you that way."

"Have you thought about me very much?" Her face sobered and her voice became huskier. "I've thought about you. A lot. I guess that's pretty standard procedure, isn't it? Schoolgirl gets crush on handsome teacher."

I swallowed with difficulty. The conversation was getting out of hand. I wasn't controlling it at all.

"We'd better get down to work," I said. "Have you thought about a subject for your term paper?"

She appraised the couch under the long window, seemed satisfied, and settled onto it with a relaxed ease and grace of movement. "Well, if we must work—" she murmured. "No, I haven't thought about it. Did you have any suggestions for me?"

"You might be interested in medieval romances," I offered, struggling to keep my mind on what I was saying. "You could do something on the tradition of courtly love."

She smiled suddenly. "I think I'd like that. Maybe you should tell me about it, Professor."

"No. That'll be your project for research."

"I have a better idea," she said softly. "I bet you know a lot about it. You could just show me."

I shifted uncomfortably on my feet. The floor of the trailer creaked audibly. Betraying me, I thought. The clumsy male shuffling his feet in embarrassment. "Laurie, I—"

"Professor, you didn't really want me to come up here to talk about a term paper, did you?"

I started at her in confusion, thrown off balance by her directness. Slowly everything came into focus. This was a strange creature, all right. But nothing other-worldly. She might be dangerous but not in the way I had feared. She was simply a sensuous, desirable woman. The feelings she inspired could hardly have been more human.

"Well, if you won't come to me," she said, "I guess I'll have to come to you."

She uncurled deliberately from the couch and swayed toward me, her body as sleek and graceful as a cat's. Even the rippling movement of flesh and muscle under the tight coverall reminded me of a cat's powerful rhythm of motion. She stopped very close to me. There was laughter in the green eyes, but as I stared into them, their shading changed, deepened. Her fingers ran up my chest to my shoulders and paused there.

"How many times do I have to ask you?" she breathed.

Control snapped like a taut wire breaking. Our lips and our bodies met, adjusting and fitting together with an instinctive familiarity. She was not one of those women who are awkward to kiss, who seem made of separate parts joined together, whose bodies never lose an indefinable tension. Her body was a single, marvelously mobile unit and it seemed made expressly for mine, at once fluid and firm, swelling and yielding, excitingly strong and meltingly soft. I felt reason sliding swiftly away from me into a crimson pool of sensation.

She pulled away from me with a violent twist. We eyed each other warily, like enemies. I felt the heavy pounding of my heart and tasted the long unfamiliar sweetness of lipstick.

"Well, Professor! I never would have thought it. Or maybe I did."

"Perhaps we should try that again," I said. "For verification."

Her eyes sparkled. "I love to be made love to in an erudite way," she said. "Make love to me, Professor."

This time she didn't have to ask twice. I reached for her but she slipped away, backing toward the couch. I caught her. For a moment she struggled and I heard breathless laughter. Then she was in my arms again, her red mouth warm and alive, and my fingers found the zipper on her suit, pulled it down the long, supple line of her back—

A pounding penetrated the haze in my brain. At first I thought it was the blood pumping furiously through my own veins but suddenly I wasn't holding her any more and she was staring beyond me toward the door.

The loud, officious knock came again.

"My God, who would that be?" she whispered.

"I don't know."

"Oh, damn, damn damn!" She jerked angrily at the zipper. "Just when my professor was warming to his subject."

I grinned and the laughter spread through me, silent exhilarating. Fear and danger seemed very remote.

"I'll tell the man to go away," I said.

I was still grinning broadly when I pulled open the door. Two uniformed policemen confronted me, their faces hard and unsmiling.

8

"I DON'T UNDERSTAND," I said.

"It's a simple question," Sgt. Bullock said, shifting his broad and solid buttocks on the small pedestal chair in front of the desk. "Do you know a girl named Lois Worthington?"

"I don't know. I know a girl named Lois, a waitress at a little restaurant near the university, But—"

"That's the one." the sergeant glanced meaningfully at his partner, who abruptly tore his gaze away from Laurie. She sat on the couch under the window, her legs drawn up under her, her face extraordinarily cool and composed under the flaming hair.

"I don't really know her," I said. "I mean, I've just met her in the Dugout."

"You don't know her very well, huh?"

"No, I—" I remembered the attempts I had made to reach her that day. The hard shrewd eyes of the policeman never left my face and I felt a chill of foreboding. "Look, Sergeant, what's this all about?"

"I understand you were trying pretty hard to get hold of the girl today. You made quite a scene about it." His eyes flicked toward Laurie, and there was a faint sneer on his flat cold face. "She another one of your students?"

"No. I was—in an accident last night. It happened right in front of the Dugout. I know Lois was on duty and I thought she might have been a witness. I wanted to ask her what she saw."

"You report this accident?"

I flushed. "No."

"Why not?"

"I—I didn't think I was hurt at the time. But today I had a painful rib and I thought I'd better make sure—"

"You thought maybe you might be able to collect a little something, eh Professor?"

I began to get angry. "Maybe I did—but that isn't what you came here to ask me about, Sergeant. If you've got something on your mind let's have it. Otherwise—"

"Don't get smart, Professor!" The sergeant rose abruptly. One jerky stride brought him close to me. The heavy face looked mean and dangerous as he thrust it in front of mine. "I'll ask the questions the way I want to ask them. And you'll listen and you'll answer, just like one of your students in the classroom, nice and polite!"

I held my tongue but I could feel the skin tighten across my cheekbones.

"Now!" he snarled. "You were in the Dugout asking for the girl between six and seven tonight. That right?"

"I left about seven-thirty."

"Yeah. And you said you'd be back later. You acted like you had a date with her."

"That's not true!"

"But you were going back."

I glanced at Laurie. There was a bright spark in her eyes as she waited for me to answer.

"Yes. I was going back."

"But instead you went to see her, didn't you, Professor?"

I showed my surprise. "No. I came straight here."

"What time did you get here?"

"Just before eight. I had an appointment—with Miss Hendricks."

"Yeah?" He whirled toward Laurie. "And what time did you get here?"

"It was five minutes past eight, Sergeant," she lied calmly. "I know because I was a few minutes late and I checked my watch."

The sergeant glared at her suspiciously, then swung back

52

to me. "You've been here since then? The two of you?"

"That's right," I said, wondering at the smoothness of Laurie's lie. "Now maybe you'll tell me what this has to do with—Miss Worthington."

His small hard eyes snapped with something like pleasure. "She was murdered, professor. That's all."

I felt the blood drain from my face. "Murdered?"

"Yeah. We figure between eight and eight-thirty, closer to eight. That's nice timing for you, professor. Seems like the girl had a helluva lot of boyfriends—but you were number one on our list!"

I stared at the hostile face and thought about what would have happened if Laurie hadn't lied, if I'd had only my own word that I was alone in the trailer between eight and nine. And then I thought about what would happen if they learned that she had lied.

But when my mind turned to Lois and why I had wanted to see her, I felt a fear that had nothing to do with the policeman's threatening attitude, a quivering fear that started way down inside me, a queasy weakness that made me feel sick.

"How—how was she killed?"

"Nice and quick, Professor. Her neck was broken."

I heard Laurie gasp and I looked at her quickly. Her face was pale now, heightening the bright red slash of her lips. Her eyes were fixed on me, wide and frightened.

The sergeant started toward the door. His partner went down the steps ahead of him. The burly man turned in the doorway.

"This lets you out for now, professor. But we'll check out your story. And maybe we'll have another little talk later on. Be around where I can find you, huh?"

"Any time, Sergeant," I said, feeling that my voice sounded hollow and unconvincing. "If there's any way I can help—"

"Yeah," he said, the flat lips stretching in what might have passed for a smile. "Sure."

He took another long, steady look at Laurie and at me

before he turned his broad back on us and went out. I waited until the two men had gone down the walk to the street before I closed the door.

Laurie hadn't moved. There was an expression in her eyes and around her mouth that I didn't immediately fathom, a curious tension. But the brutal announcement about Lois had been shocking. Small wonder that Laurie would be upset.

"Thanks, Laurie," I said. "You got me out of a spot."

"Happy to oblige," she said coldly.

I regarded her in blank surprise. "What's the matter?"

She swung off the couch and moved toward me, her walk unconsciously sensuous. "I really had you figured wrong, didn't I?" she said, her voice strangely sharp.

"Laurie, you don't think I had anything to do with—"

"No. No, I don't think you killed her. But you fooled me once, Professor, so I could be wrong again. I had you typed as the lonely professor. I bet you really got a boot out of that behind that smug face of yours, didn't you?"

"You're wrong, Laurie."

"I'll say! What were you going to do, anyway? Have a little roll on the couch with the eager student, send her on her way, and then trot along to meet your little waitress? You must be quite a guy, Professor. I should have known from the way you kissed me, shouldn't I? You didn't learn that in a book."

She was clearly hurt, a stung pride firing the bitterness of her words, and I knew she wasn't going to listen to me.

"Laurie, I had to talk to her, believe me—"

"Sure you did! About the accident, wasn't that it? You needed a witness."

"I had to ask her a question—"

"Does she always say yes? You don't have to tell me the question, Professor. I can guess. I've seen the girl!"

"I can't explain but you've got to understand that there was nothing between me and Lois."

"Tell that to the cops, Mr. Cameron. But next time don't expect me to provide your alibi!"

54

She stalked past me, jerked open the door, and bolted down the steps. I started after her.

"Laurie!"

But she was gone down the walk, the pattern of red and white diamonds twitching with the angry vehemence of her stride. And all at once it seemed too vehement to me, her anger and refusal to listen too unreasonable, a convenient way to get away quickly, just as she had been too smooth and ready to lie for me.

She had not only provided my alibi. She had created one for herself.

I heard the rumble of a voice. Looking up I saw the chunky figure of Sgt. Bullock coming down the steps of the trailer next door. Behind him light outlined the blonde hair and slim figure of the shy girl who was my neighbor. The momentary sense of safety shattered around me like a glass shell breaking. Bullock had been checking on the alibi. It had been that easy!

The sergeant was lumbering toward me. His partner stood on the walk, not moving. I waited, unable to stir. I hadn't done it, I had had nothing to do with Lois' death, but they wouldn't believe me now after the lie. I should have told them the truth.

"What's the matter, Professor? Your girl friend decide to go home early?"

"She was—upset," I said tightly.

He looked almost genial. He's enjoying this, I thought. He's going to get a big kick out of letting me have it right between the eyes.

"We checked out your alibi, Cameron," the sergeant said. "Your neighbor backs you up on the time you got here and she saw the girl arrive just after eight, so I guess we had it wrong. No hard feelings?"

"No," I said woodenly, stunned. "No, of course not."

"We'll find out who did it," the sergeant said matter-of-factly. "But now we're going to have to dig."

They left. I watched them until they had climbed into the yellow-and-black helicopter parked on the strip across the street and the ship rose slowly with a deep chugging rhythm of engine and whirring blade into the night sky. At last I turned to stare at the trailer next to mine. The door was closed. The blinds were tightly drawn. The girl had shut herself inside.

Everyone was giving me an alibi, I thought. Nobody wanted me in jail. I wondered why. The bewildering sequence of events, the jolting pile-up of shocks, had left me confused, unable to think clearly. But after a while, still standing in the open doorway looking at the blind walls of the trailer just a few yards away, I thought of a reason why.

Jails were safe.

9

I HAD ANOTHER night of fitful sleep that left me bone weary in the morning. I fought against the deep sleep that might bring a recurrence of the terrifying dream in which I was sucked down into cold black waters, and as a result I dozed and woke in momentary panic and lay sweating in bed and finally dozed again and woke again, on and on through the night. Images of dreams and reality kept getting mixed up in a disorganized montage. I would be holding Laurie in my arms, feeling the firm and vital strength of her young body warm against me, and suddenly the face which tilted up to meet mine, the lips that parted, were not hers but those of a shy and timid girl with soft blonde hair whose name I didn't know. Or I would dream fragmentarily of being trapped in a corner with the meaty face of Sgt. Bullock shoving aggressively at me and snarling, "Why did you kill her?" And, waking, I would think of Lois and ask myself why she had died, knowing in my heart that she had had to die, that I had marked her for death. Because she knew. She had seen the alien. When I had tried to find her I had become the unwitting instrument of her death. Guilt hung over me like a heavy, airless blanket, smothering me, clogging my lungs like the thick black waters of the dream. At last the gray dawn came abruptly to the crest of the mountains and found me leaden-eyed and exhausted.

It was a Friday. I had two classes that morning, including the eleven o'clock sophomore survey. Laurie Hendricks was absent. Somehow I managed to stumble through the lectures, not sure afterwards what I had said, surprised at times to find myself talking fluently with apparent coherence and logic, asking questions and answering them, functioning like a robot, well-trained to impersonate an English instructor.

And somehow it was afternoon and the last class of the day was over. I was free to return to the library. Dully, I began to read the articles and papers I had set aside the previous day. I read without hope, almost without interest, convinced that I would find nothing to explain the puzzle of the invading minds—yet believing more firmly now that they were real, not a product of my own sickness, because a woman had died who might have named them. And at length I shoved the pile of magazine and papers aside with sudden impatience.

I would find no answers here. I had to go out to find them. I could neither hide from the aliens nor attempt to outwit them, but I could force them into the open. I could attack even if I had no chance to win. One of the four students had already been tested—and I could not bring myself to believe that Laurie was still suspect. Her conduct the night before, in retrospect, seemed too clearly the actions of a lovely, spoiled young girl used to having what she wanted—and at the moment wanting me. But she was only one of four.

A sound broke the wandering circle of my thought. A footstep on a metal staircase. The library stacks were a network of crowded aisles with two levels packed into each story of the building and short connecting flights of metal stairway linking the many levels. Yet why had this footstep struck my ear? There had been movement all afternoon through the stacks as the librarians came and went.

This step was furtive, I thought. I rose slowly from the little desk under the window. The other sounds had had a normal sequence unconsciously recorded by the mind. This step had been a single isolated sound, one that was not supposed to be heard, made by a person moving stealthily and silently.

I peered along the narrow aisle which ended at the window. I was conscious of the afternoon light at my back, framing me against the window. No one was in sight, but I knew someone was there, approaching me, and I felt a now familiar flinching as fear tightened its grip.

He stepped out of a side aisle, confronting me so suddenly that it was as if he had materialized before my eyes.

"What do you want?" I asked sharply.

"I want to talk to you, Mr. Cameron," Bob Jenkins said in a low, tight voice.

"You're not supposed to be back here in the stacks."

"I told them I had to see you."

Of course, I thought. The librarians were reasonable people. How could they know why Jenkins had to see me? Why should they be suspicious? *If* he had talked to them.

Jenkins stepped forward and I saw the hard crease of his mouth, the snap of anger in narrow blue eyes. At that moment, we both heard the rapid tattoo of a woman's steps on a ladder nearby. Jenkins spun around. Bustling movement went along a nearby aisle, going away from us. When Jenkins swung back, he seemed to have relaxed slightly, though his face was still coldly unfriendly.

"Leave her alone!" he said harshly.

I gaped at him in pure astonishment.

"You know who I mean. Laurie! I know she went to your place last night."

"That—that was about a term paper assignment," I stammered.

"Don't try to kid me. I saw her when she came home

last night. She was so mad she wouldn't even talk to me—and she didn't smear her lipstick all by herself."

I began to recover from the stunning surprise of his outburst. The danger I had expected was so much more to be feared than the anger of a jealous boy that I had an hysterical impulse to laugh. But his anger seemed genuine. I think if the librarian hadn't been there in the stacks nearby he would have started a fight.

"She's my girl," Jenkins snapped. "Keep away from her!"

"That's for her to decide, isn't it?" I asked quietly. "But I don't think you have anything to worry about. I doubt that she'll want to see me again."

"Don't try to brush me off!" the boy said fiercely. "If you don't leave her alone, maybe the school would like to know about it. The authorities wouldn't like it!"

I felt a trace of answering anger. "If you're thinking of creating a scandal," I said coldly, "maybe you'd better think about Laurie's reputation too. If you try to damage me, you'll be hurting her as well."

The words shook him. He glared at me, fists clenched, breathing hard and quick as if he had been running, and I sensed the conflict in his mind, the rage made impotent.

"Damn you!" he choked. "I'm warning you. Next time I'll make you pay for it!"

He flung away down the aisle, vanishing from sight as he bolted along a connecting corridor. I could hear the harsh fall of his steps fading away from me. I took a deep breath and held it, let it out slowly, feeling some of the tension subside in my arms and legs and chest.

Chalk up another threat, I thought wearily. First vicious, powerful minds that toyed with me. Then suspicious police. Mysterious neighbors. And now a kid's jealousy so strong and blind that it could make him do something foolish. I could never get an insurance policy, I thought with a feeble attempt at humor. The odds were against my being around to pay next month's premium.

Jenkins' abrupt appearance and his jealous wrath had seemed honestly motivated. If he were one of the aliens would he have acted that way? What purpose would it serve? Then I remembered the librarian's timely interruption. Had she halted more than a threatened fist fight? Had Jenkins' plan for an accident been spoiled by the presence of someone else, forcing him to improvise a clever and plausible reason for stalking me?

No. It was probably true that he would have had to explain his purpose in order to gain access to the stacks. The librarians guarded the entrance as zealously as they undoubtedly guarded their bedroom doors. If he had planned any serious harm to me, he wouldn't have advertised his guilt. This was not the place he would have chosen.

My mind was tired of questions. Jenkins was still not removed from suspicion. No one was. I was no closer to getting any answers than I had ever been.

10

I FOUND MIKE Boyle on the practice football field at the west end of the campus. The first team was scrimmaging a group of substitutes who were running through the plays of one of the schools on the weekend's double-header. I saw Boyle roving wide to defend against an attempted end run, saw him follow the play, not moving fast, until suddenly he was charging forward, boucing off the interference in such a way that he kept his feet and sliced through to the halfback who was caught open and hemmed in near the sidelines, a sitting duck for the tackle that slammed him to the ground. And then Boyle was on his feet, amazingly nimble and springy for such a big man, trotting away without glancing back at the runner, who rose slowly and stiffly.

The deceptive ease of the play showed why Boyle was an All-American candidate. It also revealed something I had heard about the big roving tackle—whose position was one added to football's original eleven-man team in order to give the defense some needed help in the increasingly wide-open style of the game. Boyle showed an uncanny ability to divine what the opponent was going to do. Somehow, wherever a play went, he was there in front of it, anticipating it almost as if he knew precisely where it was going. The fact was an innocent one, but now it made me wonder as I watched him in action. Everything was suspect now, I thought. Nothing was innocent.

The scrimmaging continued for twenty minutes while I watched. Then the first team was called off the field for a rest and the second unit went in against the same tired group of subs. Some of the first team limbered up after the bruising workout by running up and down the sidelines. Others flipped a football or just stood watching.

I walked toward Mike Boyle. As I neared him he gulped water from a ladle dipped into a pail and spewed it out in a great gusher. Then he drank, his throat working visibly, sweat pouring down his face to mix with the water that spilled around his mouth and ran down his throat. He seemed to do everything in a big, robust way. In the padded uniform, he appeared immense, twice as broad as I and towering over me. He had not seemed nearly as big in street clothes.

I stood waiting while he drank. I was sure that he had not noticed my approach but he spoke as he dropped the ladle into the pail.

"Hi, Prof. Been running into any more cars?"

"I manage to keep out of the way of most of them."

He grinned. His mouth was full lipped and wide, matching the proportions of a prominent nose that had once been broken and an unruly mass of black hair. Only the eyes were too small for the face, but that might have been due to the habitual squint against the sun of a young man who spent a great deal of his time outdoors.

"You professors kill me," Boyle said. "What was on your mind, Prof? A poem or something?"

"Something I heard."

"Yeah? It must have been good," he said offhandedly, "to

make you walk in front of the only damn car on the street."

"It was," I said.

The small brown eyes regarded me curiously and I wondered if their glint held amusement or something deeper.

"Well, you better be careful," Boyle said. "Hearing things like that won't do you any good if you're dead."

I read menace into the words, but it was belied by the faintly contemptuous grin on his face. He had the habitual cockiness which I had often seen in the professional campus athlete to whom public adulation has come too soon, before the mind is mature enough to discount it. The attitude was always irritating.

"That's a nice looking girlfriend of yours," I said, perhaps too casually. "Isn't she a physics major?"

"Helen? Yeah, she's a brain," he agreed. "A cute kid, though," he added, as if the combination of cuteness and intelligence was cause for surprise. "We have a ball."

"Miss Hendricks said you were going steady."

"Yeah? You might say that, Prof. But I'm not the kind of guy that likes to be tied down. You know?"

I was groping, trying to find a way to ask him where he had been the night before without seeming to be probing. I found myself disliking the youthful arrogance and it was an effort to keep the amiably stupid smile on my lips. I stood for a moment in silence, watching the scrimmage. The subs executed an intricate play that caught the defense completely out of position for the pass. Boyle cursed vehemently.

"They should have smelled that one a mile off," he growled.

"Doesn't the coach object when you go out on dates during the week?" I asked suddenly. "Or do you have a curfew?"

He spat vigorously. "Nuts," he said. "I'm his bread and butter. I go out when I want to."

I hesitated. "I thought I saw you and Helen again last night," I said. "Pretty late, too. I was on my way home from a movie."

He swung around slowly and the small brown eyes caught mine in a fixed stare. The indefinable trace of contempt marked the expression of his eyes and mouth.

"Prof," he said softly, "you didn't see me and Helen out last night. You got something on your mind. Maybe you should tell me what it is."

"I guess I was mistaken," I said, glad at that moment that I had had the sense to pick this time and place to sound him out, with a hundred people in clear view and within shouting distance. I was not sure what the hint of ugliness in his voice and manner signified. The thickly-muscled chest and arms didn't frighten me. Rather it was the thought of this brutal strength directed by a supremely powerful intelligence.

"Yeah, you made a mistake, Prof. Helen was with me last night but you didn't see us. I tell you what. You want to know if Helen was with me last night, you just go ask her, huh? And don't bother me with your nosy questions."

"I can assure you I wasn't being nosy," I said in my best and huffiest imitation of professorial dignity. "I was merely making conversation."

"Sure you were. Well, you just go talk to yourself, Prof. Only watch out for those cars. We'd miss you around here."

He turned his back on me and began to do a series of leg exercises, squatting and jumping erect, thick thighs stretching the pants of his uniform each time he dropped into the crouch.

I walked away slowly. The momentary irritation I felt over the open contempt shown by a muscle-headed athlete was not important. But if his statement about being with Helen Darrow could be believed, it was highly significant. It meant that they could vouch for each other, providing that they were together at the time Lois Worthington was killed. Boyle was the one suspect I knew who could easily have broken the girl's neck without even breathing hard. But I was convinced that Lois' death was linked to the aliens and I knew there were not three of them. There was the man who had been in the back booth and one student.

63

Not two. Helen Darrow could prove that both she and Mike Boyle were innocent. In one stroke the possible number of suspects would be cut in half.

11

I FELT A compulsion to keep moving. Even the negative results I had garnered so far gave me a feeling of accomplishing something. In addition I was avoiding being a fixed target. The fact that the aliens had not already struck again surprised me. Almost two full days had passed since the first hastily improvised attempt on my life. It was not comforting to reflect that they would want to be absolutely sure of me the second time—and it was probably not easy to arrange a foolproof accident.

Besides—came the chilling thought—they had been busy the night before with Lois Worthington.

I needed greater mobility. That meant a car. I rented a small closed aluminum model from a lot near the university. While the cost was high, I seemed to have acquired a new indifference to economics. Whether I ate next week or paid next month's rent didn't seem to matter any more. My entire perspective had gradually been changing. Even the conditioned obedience to academic rules of propriety was disappearing. Twenty-four hours before I had been reluctant to seek Lois' address from the registrar's office, afraid that my motive might be questioned. That had cost the girl her life. Now I had no hesitation about going to the office for the two addresses I wanted. Ironically, the girl behind the counter didn't even appear curious. I wouldn't have cared if she had.

Was this the schizophrenic's apathy, his progressive lack of orientation? There were gaps in the days when I had done habitual things like shaving and changing clothes. I couldn't remember doing them. The car's mirror reflected an image that could have been someone else, a young man whose face showed little evidence of strain and fatigue. In fact, despite my lack of sleep, I didn't feel tired. I felt as if I had been wound up tight and any minute I would be released and would begin to spin madly.

Madly. The word stuck. It kept coming back, the awful fear. My stumbling investigations had a double-edged motive: to find the aliens—and to prove that I was not mad. And I was slowly, inexorably, trapping myself in a narrowing circle. If I sat back, if I did nothing, I wouldn't know for sure. I could believe in mysterious beings from outer space, in sinister plots against me, in the hallucination of bodiless voices. I wouldn't have to confront unpleasant implications about morbid attempts at self-destruction or a disintegrating personality.

Even during the twenty-seven years of my life, society had come a long way in its attitude toward insanity. No longer was it viewed with a sense of shame or revulsion, something to be ignored or swept into a corner of society where you didn't have to look at it. But it was still the nation's number one disease, it still inspired the terror of the unknown. We had had many scientific breakthroughs—the famous virus break in 1971 which meant the end of cancer, the virtual elimination of the common cold; the successful "heart patch" of 1975 which changed heart disease from a leading killer to a rarely fatal disease; the total elimination of polio and multiple sclerosis and many other vicious enemies of the human organism. But the mind remained impregnable.

There had been gigantic strides in treatment, but mental hospitals were still jammed far beyond capacity. One American in five had some form of mental illness. Some, the luckier ones, found quick cures in the K7U drugs available under prescription, the laboratory narcotic that had proved startlingly effective, enabling you to induce exaggerated symptoms of psychoses under their influence, thus making possible an accurate diagnosis that could lead to prompt treatment. But there had been many cases of alarming toxic side effects from K7U. And in one area of mental illness the miracle drug had quite a different result. It accelerated the advanced stages of paranoid schizophrenia and its rarer, more logically organized cousin, paranoia.

There was a small bottle of K7U pills in the top drawer of the built-in chest in my trailer bedroom, a supply I had surreptitiously borrowed from the psychology laboratory when I first became aware of what seemed hallucinatory voices. I had been afraid to use them. If mine were a minor illness, the pills would expose it to accurate treatment. There was the risk of side effects but that did not deter me. My symptoms did.

The hallucination of voices where no one was present was a common one. It was frequently allied to a fairly well organized delusional system in which the person held the bizarre conviction that supra-human beings were trying to possess or destroy him—and often was convinced that he himself had some extraordinary powers that accounted for the persecution. He might seem quite normal in other phases of his life, well-oriented to his surroundings except for a tendency to withdraw socially, avoiding close personal relationships, and an increasing emotional apathy sometimes alternating with moments of exaggerated feeling.

This symptomatic pattern was common in paranoid schizophrenia.

Grimly I thrust aside the conclusion to which my thoughts had led me, ignoring the tight stomach cramp of fear, pretending that the reason for panic did not exist.

I was heading south through the Culver basin, the west end of the city's sprawling complex of trailer courts that ranged from the utilitarian government projects for low income dwellings to luxurious resort-like courts. I stayed off the automatic drive freeways, preferring to control the car manually even though it meant a slower trip. I needed contact with busy, noisy, normal humanity.

Moving on the ground level streets through the trailer basin gave me a viewpoint I had not had in two years. I had lived in the basin with my mother up to the time of her death. Afterwards I had obeyed the inclination to cut myself off from everything and everyone I had known. I had been fortunate in finding the vacancy in the court off Mulholland Drive. In a city of sixteen million people forever bursting out of their housing, that had been an even luckier chance than I had realized. There was already a public clamor to re-zone Beverly Hills for apartments and middle-income trailer courts. It was the city's last remaining area of private homes and only the vast wealth and influence of the rich and politically powerful who lived there had kept it from being overwhelmed by the creeping mass of trailers and great apartment cities.

Now, viewing the basin after a long absence, I could see the smothering effects of overcrowding. The sidewalks were so jammed that people had to move in funereal procession. At those rare cross streets where there was not a pedestrian underpass there were three minute intervals while cars waited for the surging wave of pedestrians to flow across the street. Automobile traffic was heavy in spite of the great numbers who no longer drove, preferring to take the speedy elevated trains which thundered overhead at frequent intervals. And over the whole area there was an unending murmur of sound, of feet and horns and voices and loudspeakers of public telescreens and taped music, the whole orchestra of sound like the unending drone that would exist in the center of a giant beehive. And the city smelled. It smelled of sweat and oil and seared meat and smoke and French perfumes. It smelled of humanity penned into a seemingly airless enclosure. I had the feeling of being imprisoned within solid walls of sound and smell and motion.

The world was fast becoming much too small. Over twenty-five years of uninterrupted peace had combined with the achievements of science against sickness and disease and accident to produce a vast population explosion with all of its attendant overcrowding and unemployment and food shortages. The world needed space. Already the crime rate was climbing alarmingly. Traditional food resources were being exhausted.

We needed the universe to grow in. But what enemies lay waiting for us on those distant planets circling through the void? Was it conceivable that I, alone in all the world, had met the first of those enemies? That I held the fate of mankind in my hands? Would anyone believe me if I could warn those who might save us?

No. They wouldn't listen. An overcrowded world had produced a surplus of fanatic prophets of doom. They would be sympathetic, the leaders who might hear my cry of warning. If I got violent, they would forcibly confine me for treatment. But if what I believed was not madness but reality, and if I failed to stop the aliens, humanity would perish.

Absorbed in thought I missed the intersection I was searching for. In no time, I was lost in the maze. The street pattern was so chaotic that, even with a map, it took me an hour to find what I sought, the Lucky Galaxy Trailer Court. By then it was dusk and I realized I would probably be arriving just at dinner time.

I wondered what the Darrows would be like.

The trailer was quite old, slightly larger than my own, set on its own small plot of ground with a tiny cement patio and several square yards of grass and garden, carefully tended. In spite of its age, the trailer had a look of well-scrubbed cleanliness and perfect repair, an air of privacy and pride. I remembered my mother's attempts to keep our trailer clean and comfortable and homelike, and how restless and ill at ease she had felt in the newer trailer we had bought after my father's legacy to her, a modern trailer made of materials that shone without cleaning, full of gadgets that made cooking effortlessly impersonal and housework obsolete.

The blinds were not drawn in the Darrow trailer. I could see a man of middle age standing in the living room before a three-dimensional TV screen. He had his arm cocked in the pose of a football player about to throw a pass. In the kitchen a plump little woman moved back and forth busily, her back toward me. I saw no sign of Helen Darrow as I went up the short walk to the door.

The man answered my knock. He had a short, spare figure and defeated eyes surrounded by wrinkles that suggested he had once laughed a great deal. He carried his shoulders erect and square with a suggestion of defiant pride. At the moment the corners of his mouth were pulled down in an expression of irritation. "What is it? he snapped.

"Is Helen in?" I asked.

Curiosity stirred in the dull eyes. "Nope. But she'll be back in a few minutes. We're just about to eat," he added pointedly.

"Ask the young man in," a voice called from within the trailer.

"Well, I don't want to interrupt your dinner," I said. "I just wanted to talk to your daughter for a few minutes."

"Nonsense," the woman said, appearing suddenly beside the man. "Come right in."

I hesitated. The man turned his back on me and trotted back to the TV screen. The woman beamed cheerfully at me. I stepped inside, feeling uncomfortable about my mission.

"My name is Cameron," I said awkwardly. "I—I'm an instructor at the university."

"Well, isn't that nice, George? He's one of Helen's teachers."

"No, I'm not," I said quickly. "But I know her and—"

"Won't you stay for dinner? Have you eaten?"

"I couldn't do that."

"Rubbish," Mrs. Darrow said brightly. "There's plenty, and it's always nice to have a guest when you're a good cook. And I am," she added with unaffected pleasure.

I smiled. The odors of fresh vegetables cooking filled the small room. "I'll bet you are," I said. "But I can't stay. I have another call to make."

"You have to stop to eat sometime," she said placidly,

69

ignoring my protests and getting another plate from the built-in rack.

There was an unexpected thump from the living area. I turned to see George Darrow rising from the couch and going through the motions of dusting himself off. His eyes glittered with pleasure. I heard the announcer's voice from the TV set talking excitedly about someone just getting a pass away before being dumped. The pass was complete for a fifteen yard gain. With a faint smile, I realized that Darrow was one of those millions of sports addicts who lived for the synthetic participation games so popular now on television.

"You can eat while you're talking to Helen," Mrs. Darrow said behind me. "Unless it's private, of course. . . ."

"No," I said quickly. "I really shouldn't be bothering her but I thought she might be able to help me."

"You just go into the living room with father. Helen'll be here any minute. George, isn't that game over yet?"

"We're in the last quarter," George Darrow said excitedly. "Watch that safety man!"

I was in time to see a pass skip off the oustretched fingers of a defensive halfback. Darrow sighed with heartfelt relief.

"That was close," he muttered. "We're playing the New York Bruins," he added. "I'm with the Toronto Titans tonight."

I took a seat at the side of the room so as not to get in the little man's way. It was remarkable how his eyes had lost their lifelessness. They were avid, greedy with interest. He bent forward eagerly, calling imaginary signals under his breath. The ball was snapped and it seemed to spiral directly toward us in the startling illusion of the dimensional screen. George Darrow reached to gather it in and faded back a couple of steps to pass, looking for a receiver. The announcer's voice rose in an animated description of the action.

I thought of the billions of men and sports-crazy youngsters throughout the world who would be duplicating his actions, just as he imitated the movements of the passer on the screen now, taking the passer's place through the trickery of the television cameras. The participation sports events provided a year round diet of baseball and football, hockey and jai alai, and various other games and contests in which the viewer could have the vicarious thrill of taking part. I had never enjoyed them. I could only contrast the closed, air-conditioned, private sports arenas, where the professional athletes played before the eyes of the cameras alone, with the noisy confusion of the stadiums I remembered from my childhood, where teams battled before live audiences, where you saw the action itself and not an illusion of it.

But George Darrow's sports enthusiasm might prove useful to me. He would probably not be at all reluctant to talk about Mike Boyle. I waited impatiently for the game to end. Except for the announcer's voice with its false excitement and George Darrow's quick breathing and occasional grunts, the trailer's peace was disturbed only by the small, familiar kitchen sounds of a woman preparing a family meal, happy in the surprise addition of a guest. The place was full of her warmly sentimental touches—frilly draperies, hand-crafted artifacts, an elaborately framed telephone screen in rare genuine maple. My own trailer in comparison was bare and cold and impersonal. I began to feel more keenly the absurdity of any suspicion that this warm and modest home, so typically human, could house an unearthly creature.

George Darrow pressed a chair button to turn off the TV set. The game was over. The room was abruptly silent. He sank into a chair, staring at me. After a moment he coughed, seemed about to speak, thought better of it.

"You must know Mike Boyle pretty well," I said casually.

The man's eyes brightened again. "Mike? Sure do. Best roving tackle in the country, that boy."

I had struck the chord. "Yes. I saw Mike this afternoon

71

scrimmaging. A couple of tough games coming up this weekend."

"We'll take 'em," Darrow said. "Mike should make All-American in a walk, the kind of season he's having. He's the difference in our team." He paused, then looked up happily. "Mike and Helen are going steady, you know."

"Yes, I knew. That reminds me, did Helen see him last night? I heard the coach talked to him about being out late, again, breaking training."

Darrow laughed. "They may talk to Mike but he don't listen. He does just what he wants, that boy. Yeah, he and Helen had a date last night. Like most nights. But they weren't out late, were they, mother?"

Mrs. Darrow carried a steaming bowl over to the table at one end of the kitchen. "I'd say about eleven," she said. "Mike's a good boy, Mr. Cameron. I never worry when Helen is out with him."

"I'm glad to hear that," a voice broke in.

We all turned toward the door. The slender brunette I had seen with Boyle stood in the doorway watching me, her face unsmiling.

I rose. "We were just talking about you."

"I heard."

She took a couple of steps into the room, her eyes still sharply observant, and I wondered whether there was anything of wariness in them—or just a girl's natural suspicion of a stranger who comes around asking questions.

"Mr. Cameron stopped by to see you," her mother said cheerfully, "so I asked him to stay for dinner. It's all ready."

"Maybe he doesn't have time," the girl suggested.

"He has to eat," the woman said, briskly appraising my tall, angular frame. "And he looks like he could use a good, home-cooked meal."

I smelled the heaping bowl of vegetables and the thick slices of real bread. Sharp teeth of hunger gnawed at me.

"I guess I am hungry at that."

72

Although it was obvious that she did not welcome my presence, Helen Darrow did not object, nor did she press immediately to find out what I wanted to see her about. The four of us sat around the small table and ate. The girl and her father were silent. Mrs. Darrow talked with unaffected garrulousness about Helen and her aspirations in physics, her childhood successes in school, the happiness she had brought her parents. Pride bloomed in the mother's voice. The girl would sometimes smile slightly and make a mild protest which her mother brushed aside. I began to realize that the girl was not actively unfriendly, simply reserved and rather serious by disposition. Soon I was feeling quite comfortable with the intimate family group. I liked them and even envied them a little. Any suspicions I might have had evaporated. When the girl's question came at last, near the end of the meal, voiced casually as if it were not important, I felt guilty about persisting in a pointless investigation. At the same time, I had to come up with a plausible excuse for my visit.

"What was it you wanted to see me about, Mr. Cameron?"

I hesitated. "You remember that accident I had the other night?"

"Of course."

"You were in an accident?" Mrs. Darrow asked with quick concern.

"Nothing serious," I said. "But I wanted to get in touch with the man who was driving the car and I seem to have lost his address. I wondered if by any chance you remember it."

Helen Darrow frowned. "Harrison, I think his name was." She seemed to accept my explanation without question. "Albert or Alfred or something like that."

"Do you remember the address?"

"Noooo. No, I can't help you there, I'm afraid."

I smiled appreciatively. "Well, it was worth a try. Maybe one of the others will remember it. I tried to phone you last night," I added with a studied lack of emphasis. "Around eight. But you must have been out."

"I was with Mike. We went out to dinner."

"That's funny," her mother said. "Father and I were in all evening."

There was an awkward silence.

"No, we weren't," George Darrow said abruptly. "We went over to the Wallaces for a few minutes. Just about eight o'clock it was."

"That must have been when I called," I said with relief. I rose from the table. "I hate to eat and run, and I do appreciate your hospitality, Mrs. Darrow, but—"

"Won't you stay and have some coffee?"

"No, I have some other calls to make. I wish I could."

"Well, you must come again."

"I'll try to do that. It isn't often I get a chance to eat a meal like this."

The girl followed me to the door. "I hope you can find the man," she said, more openly friendly now than she had been in the beginning. More at ease, I thought, liking her, liking the serious, intent face and the quiet, intelligent eyes.

"I thought you were going to ask me about that girl who was killed," she said.

I felt an involuntary tension. "No. You heard about that?"

"It was all over school today."

I relaxed. Of course it would have been a sensational topic of conversation on the campus. I could imagine the speculations, the arguments, the macabre jokes.

"A terrible thing," I said automatically. I turned to leave. "Thanks for your trouble. And thank your parents for me again."

I went out into the cool night. The girl stood watching me, a small slim figure outlined against the warm light within the trailer.

Once again my search had been fruitless. And now I had

talked to all four of the students who were in the booth of the Dugout that fateful night.

I couldn't believe that any one of them was capable of inhuman powers. Or of murder.

12

WHEN I DIALED Laurie Hendricks' number a male servant answered. The number was a Beverly Hills exchange. The man informed me politely that Miss Hendricks was not at home but that she might be reached at the beach trailer. This was the first I knew of a place at the beach, but its existence was in keeping with the expensive luxury of space I could glimpse on the telephone screen as I talked to the servant. At that moment, I made a mental connection I had failed to reach before, coupling the name Hendricks with the economy two-passenger helicopter that had brought flying within the reach of the average family's budget. The Hendricks helicopter! The name was so familiar that I had not thought to link it with Laurie Hendricks, but the wealth evident in the existence of a private home in Beverly Hills plus a beach trailer suggested that she might indeed be the daughter of Ben Hendricks, air pioneer extraordinary.

The servant gave me the address and phone number of the beach trailer. Laurie answered on the fourth ring.

"Hello?"

Her image leaped onto the screen. She was dripping wet, her red hair clinging to her head in dark, heavy strands. I glimpsed behind her a damp bathing suit tossed carelessly over the arm of a chair. She held a huge beach towel in front of her chest with one hand pressed between her breasts, the towel draping itself tantalizingly over the full-ness on either side of her hand.

"Laurie? This is Paul Cameron."

I flicked the two-way switch so that she could view me

on her screen. There was a moment's pause while her eyes stared steadily at me from the lifelike image. I wondered if she was aware that the picture was turned on at her end of the line, or if she was always so careless about dress when she answered the phone.

"What do you want?" Her voice was cool, distant.

"We were interrupted the other night."

"Were we?"

"I've got to talk to you."

"I don't think we have anything to talk about."

"I'm coming out there. Will you be waiting?"

"You needn't bother. I have a date tonight—with Bob. I have to get ready now so you must excuse me."

"You're going to listen to me whether you want to or not," I said, suddenly angry. "There was nothing for you to worry about between me and Lo—"

"Why should I worry?"

She broke the connection. In the instant before the image faded she turned away. There was nothing to conceal the sculptured beauty of her back. I stared at the screen long after it had turned blank, wondering if this brief provocative display had been another moment of absent-minded indifference or a deliberate taunt.

It had destroyed the effect of her cold rejection.

I took the automatic freeway to the beach, setting the controls for the fast inner lane. I sat back while the electronic fingers automatically steered the car safely and smoothly into the lane and carried it forward at the set speed of a hundred and fifty miles an hour.

Thinking of Laurie's image on the screen, remembering the feel of her body and her soft lips pressing against mine, I felt a slow uncurling of desire. When I had obtained her address that afternoon, I had been methodically determined to follow up every possible avenue of suspicion. She had been too quick to throw herself at me in my trailer the night before, I had argued, too ready to provide me with an alibi when the police came. Now I knew that I had simply been deceiving myself. I had eliminated her from suspicion even before I tasted the human passion of her lips. I was going to her now because I needed her. I wanted to hold her and to lose myself in her, to forget fear and threats and self-tormenting doubts of my own sanity in the intense oblivion of love.

The westbound freeway reached the intersection of the automatic ocean causeway. I made the necessary instrument adjustments and shot out over the water onto the broad cement lanes that followed the coastline to the north, a modern eight lane platform suspended on pilings a quarter mile from the shore. There was a manual drive highway just inland from the beach for slow and local traffic, but if you wanted to make speed you took the causeway out over the—

It struck me like a blow below the belt. Water! The dream! A senseless, terrorized animal, I found myself scrabbling at the door, trying to force it open. The same automatic controls which guided the car along the road also froze the doors while the car was in motion. I came out of that first blind moment of panic and sat rigid in the seat, my eyes fixed on the white ribbon of pavement directly in front of me, refusing to look to either side at the black, pounding surf. Headlights rushed at me on the inbound lanes and hurtled past. The engine whined and wind buffeted the speeding car, but I imagined that I could hear above these sounds the crash of waves below me.

Revulsion came, bitter self-recrimination, contemptuous denunciations of my own animal fears. You're going to see Laurie, I told myself. There's nothing to be afraid of. You won't have to go near the water. You won't be alone. The nightmare of drowning is a phantom of the night, symbolical only, a graphic representation of your subconscious fear of sanity. Face it. Recognize it. Accept it.

But the voice, I thought. The voice of command. The alien mind. That is real. I have heard it while I was awake and fully rational. That was no dream symbol. That was real.

77

But was it? Hadn't I investigated every one of the suspects, the four ordinary young people who were supposed to be possessed by some incredible thing from Mars? Hadn't I convinced myself that each one was innocent? Wasn't it about time that I began facing the irrefutable facts, admitting that the weird plot against me was a fantastic concoction of a sick imagination, revealing a not very unusual hidden desire for self-destruction?

I grew calmer. In that moment the terror of insanity seemed less horrifying than the spectre of a vicious alien force that could possess and destroy me. At last I looked toward the shoreline at the familiar sight of waves rising to a white crest and toppling over to wash upon the beach. I had seen this a thousand times. It was nothing to be afraid of. It couldn't touch me.

I was nearing the stretch of beach where Laurie's trailer should be. Numbers flashed by at each of the ramps connecting the causeway with the shoreline road. I pushed the lane change button that would shift the car into the slower outer line of traffic. At the next ramp I turned off. The automatic controls cut off as soon as the car sped onto the ramp. My hands were sticky on the wheel and my arms quivered with tension, but seconds later I was turning onto the beach highway. I began to feel safer now that there was no longer any water under me.

The road rose and dipped with the curvature of the land. Crowding the hills to the right, on the inland side of the road, were luxurious beach apartments and nests of trailer courts, their lights creating a rich pattern in the darkness. Most of the choice land along the beach itself had been usurped by beach clubs and expensive resort hotels, except for an occasional luxury group of trailers. It was in one of these, the Beachcomber Trailer Lodge, that Laurie's trailer had a uniquely desirable front row site.

I parked off the road on a bluff overlooking the trailer village and the beach. Walking down, I could hear the rolling thunder of the surf, and each reverberating crash caused my body to flinch in the way that, watching a fight, you will seem to feel the thud of a telling blow. I tried not to think about the limitless black plain of water stretching beyond the narrow strip of beach.

Laurie's was a crisply modern mobile home with a large window facing the shoreline. Most of the surrounding trailers were dark and there was the stillness of the empty and unused about them. There were few cars about and only a couple of helicopters on the landing strip near the road. This was mostly a weekend resort, I concluded, for those who could afford the extreme luxury of a home in town and a summer or weekend hideout at the beach. At this season of the year, many of them were undoubtedly deserted.

I knocked. There was no sound from within the trailer. I raised my hand to knock again at the moment the door was pulled open.

Laurie stiffened. "You! I told you not to come."

"And I said I had to talk to you."

She started to close the door but I shoved through. The door slammed behind me.

She held herself stiff with anger, her small fists clenched, but even the rigidity of her body could not change the curving softness of breast and hip and thigh to which the pale green tissue of her dress clung. Confronting her in the small room, I felt the same quick surge of desire, the same overpowering response to her beauty that had swept over me the night before when her physical presence had seemed to dominate the confined space of my own trailer. I had never reacted to a woman so immediately and so forcefully.

How much of my reaction showed in the way I stared at her I don't know, but it seemed to me that the bright spark of anger in her green eyes subtly altered.

"I'm not sure what you're trying to prove," she said, less sharply than I had expected, "but this isn't the way. You can leave right now."

"No. I'm here and you're going to listen to me."

Abruptly she turned away, scooping up a light coat from the back of a chair. She started toward the door.

"If you want to talk, there's a restaurant not far up the road. Maybe the waitress will listen."

I caught her arm. "I had to talk to Lois," I said, my fingers digging into the soft flesh of her arm. "It was important and I can't explain why. But I never saw her except in the Dugout, I never went out with her, I never made a pass at her."

Laurie's face was still aloof, indifferent. "Is that supposed to mean something to me?"

"Yes!"

"What do I do now—start to melt?"

"Are you trying to tell me that what happened last night meant nothing to you? Just another lark?"

She wrenched free. "What did you expect? You didn't really believe that bit about the student having a crush on teacher, did you? I was having some fun, Professor. And tonight I'm having it with someone else!"

I almost hit her. Rage rocketed through me with an explosiveness that was so shockingly violent I barely held the arm drawn back for the blow. And in the next instant I had pinned her against the wall and my arms were tightening around her, my mouth imprisoning hers in a brutal, angry kiss that brought the taste of blood to my lips. I wasn't even aware whether or not she was struggling. I knew only that she was intensely, excitingly desirable and that the full warm length of her was pressed against me.

I stepped back, breathing hard and quick. There was a frozen moment of time suspended while I waited for her to explode.

Laurie laughed. "My God, Professor, you certainly do keep surprising me!"

She tossed the coat she had been holding in the direction of the chair. It missed and tumbled onto the floor. Ignoring it, she was already moving back into my arms.

"Let's try that again," she murmured. "But this time don't bite."

The kiss was long and deeply disturbing. When it ended I felt shaky. I wanted her—but for the first time I wondered if my emotional attraction to her went beyond that need, if I wasn't already completely in love with her. I stared at the puffed redness of her bruised lips, at the delicate bone structure beneath the smooth skin of her cheeks, at the vivid coloring of her eyes, and the painful knowledge came to me that I was not free to love, not until I knew—

"I—I think I'm a little afraid of you, Paul Cameron," she said in a voice that was younger, more subdued, less self-assured than I had ever heard it. "I think you'd better leave now."

"But—"

"Please! It was true what I said about Bob—I do have a date with him. He should have been here by now." Her eyes were pleading. "I was mad at you. Besides—" she hesitated, her gaze searching my face as if she wanted to remember every line. "I think I need a little while to mull this over. This little girl isn't used to being swept off her feet. Not like this."

I reached for her but she backed away quickly. "No! Let's—let's see how we feel tomorrow when we're both a day older and wiser and—calmer. I'll be here—waiting for you."

At last I nodded. "You're right, Laurie. But if you let that blond kid—"

She smiled. "I can handle Bob."

She didn't move as I went to the door. Before I opened it her words came softly and with a surprising note of tenderness. "Goodnight—darling."

13

THE TRAILER WAS in a slight hollow. From inside, you could see the white froth along the shore, but when you stepped down to the sand outside, a smooth ridge cut off the view of the water. I could hear the smash of a breaker coming in, the receding rattle as it washed back over a bed of stones. The sound didn't frighten me now. For the moment the dream had been forgotten. Laurie's last words drifted on the cool night air, bringing their own tingling warmth.

He struck out of darkness.

I had a split second of warning, time enough to flinch against the whiplash of command. It didn't come. The shadow that had moved around the corner of the trailer closed in on me swiftly, but the blow was not a sickening mental force. It was a clumsily swinging fist that skidded painfully off my shoulder as I dodged. I heard a choking sob.

"Damn you!"

The white blob of a fist arched toward me and smashed against my jaw. I was caught off balance. Falling, I had a strange floating sensation. My cheek was numb. Even on the soft sand, the fall was jolting, and for a second I couldn't move. The figure stood panting over me and I saw blond hair caught in the slanting light from Laurie's window.

"Get up!" he raged. "Damn you, get up and fight!"

I laughed. Fear fell away from me and the reaction of relief was so intense that there was no room for anger or pain or even surprise. Jenkins! The jealous youth who had warned me to keep away from his girl.

The laughter enraged him even more. He dove on top of me. I rolled as his lean hard body slammed against me. His fingers tore at my chest, reaching for my throat. I fought back automatically, not really wanting to fight, desiring merely to stop this foolishness, yet instinctively defending myself. My flailing arm banged against the side of his head. He grunted. For an instant the pressure of his hold weakened. I wrenched free and tumbled away from him.

He came to his feet more quickly than I did. I was still in a crouch when he stepped in and brought up his knee in a short, vicious piston stroke. It exploded against my chin. My head snapped back and I toppled backwards like a limber doll.

"I'll kill you!" he snarled.

Still I felt neither anger nor fright. There was a fleeting

sense of alarm, of recognition that here was a real threat, something that had to be stopped, not just a laughable mistake. And there was pain. Blood filled my mouth and my jaw was bruised and throbbing. But everything was clear and rational and without emotion.

Somehow I got to my feet again. Absurdly the thought crossed my mind that he wasn't playing the game according to the rules. You weren't supposed to kick a man when he was down, you shouldn't use your knee at all. Then there was no more time for reflection. He rushed at me, fists pumping, and I managed to sidestep. He whirled and came at me again. His fist grazed the top of my head. I punched back, hitting for the vulnerable stomach, hoping only to slow him down. I wasn't breathing very well and I was aware of blood streaming from my nose.

We fought standing up now, without speaking, the thud of a blow echoed by a grunt or a gasp, our breathing loud and wheezing. My arms began to feel leaden where they had caught the heavy impact of his fists.

"Don't be a damned fool!" I gasped.

"I warned you!"

I was wearing down, like a mechanical doll wound up and now nearing the end of its dance, beginning to slow, each jerky movement more labored, more artificial. He was younger, in better condition, harder, stronger, more rested. I saw the end coming. His blows broke through my barriers of elbow and shoulder more frequently. He must have sensed that I was weakening and he pressed his attack more savagely.

I went down again, not so much from one blow as from an accumulation of them. The thought came dimly to me that I had no hope of winning because my heart wasn't in it. I didn't care. I had no sense of being a warrior battling for my love against the evil knight. I was apathetic. I fought only because I had to defend myself. It had nothing to do with Laurie, nothing to do with courage or honor.

Without knowing how or why, I was on my feet again, aiming for the flat hard stomach, oblivious of the knotted fist that slashed across my cheek as I drove in, not knowing why I persisted in this futile form of resistance.

A scream ripped across the darkness. Out of the corner of my eye I saw Laurie standing in a pool of light at the front of the trailer. The cry must have stopped Jenkins. I was already driving in, smashing my fist into the only target I knew, the unguarded stomach. He gave a short, emphatic grunt.

Laurie cried out again and rushed toward us. Jenkins sagged backwards and sat down hard. I stood over him, swaying, and spat blood onto the sand.

"My God! What are you doing, Paul? Why?"

"He started it," I mumbled childishly.

Jenkins said nothing. He sat where he had dropped, doubled over, his fists pressed into his stomach. I heard a strangled sound as he tried to suck air into his lungs.

Laurie began to cry. I stared at her stupidly. It seemed to be too much trouble to speak again.

"You—you bully!" she choked through tears. "Why did you have to fight him? You didn't have to!"

It would take too long to explain. She really ought to understand that I hadn't wanted to fight. I couldn't explain it all to her now.

She sank to her knees beside Jenkins. "Oh, Bob," she said soothingly. "You're hurt." She glared up at me. "Why do you always have to spoil things? Just when everything was so perfect, why—oh, go away! I never want to see you again!"

She held him gently, pressing his bent head against her bosom like a mother cradling her child. I wanted to tell her that he wasn't really hurt. I was the one who was hurt. Every bone in my body was broken. He'd only had the breath knocked out of him.

But I knew she wouldn't listen, and the effort of trying to convince her didn't seem worthwhile. Nothing mattered. I was dead tired and aching and very old.

Turning, I staggered away across the sand.

14

I SAT IN the little aluminum car for a long time. I don't know how long. The numbness slowly left my chest and arms and face, clearing the way for a thousand jabbing needles of pain. But the emotional numbness, the dull apathy, remained.

A fight shouldn't wreck you like this, I thought. At twenty-seven you aren't exactly an old man. Weren't you supposed to reach your physical peak at that age?

Why had I felt no real anger? The unemotional, automatic resistance during the fight was abnormal. My feeling now of being drained and empty was disproportionate. A reaction to the weeks of strain, perhaps, with the physical beating I had taken providing the finishing blows.

Or did it go deeper than that? My reaction to Laurie was not normal either. The emotional pendulum was swinging far too wide at both ends of its arc. I was not a kid any more, not an unstable adolescent. Kissing a young and beautiful girl was not a unique, soul-shattering experience. The moment's passion with Laurie had meant too much. Granted she was no ordinary girl, and in my self-imposed isolation I had not been leading what could be called a full and satisfying sex life. Yet neither of these facts seemed to account fully for the highly charged, volatile reaction I had had to her on the two occasions we had been alone for a few minutes.

Could she be exercising some unnatural influence?

As I examined the thought a feeling of disgust welled up in me. It won't work, I thought dully, the revulsion itself a gray, listless emotion. Laurie is dangerous only if you're afraid of love, timid in the face of a strong relationship. She is not a monster. Nor is Jenkins. He had his opportunity right there on the beach in the darkness. It would have been easy for him to use the brutal force of a super-mind instead of awkward fists. He could have done it before Laurie heard the sounds of fighting and came out. It could have been done as it was in the dream. "Drown! Drown yourself!" And no one would have known how or why it happened.

No. Not Jenkins, not Laurie, not Helen Darrow or Mike Boyle. It had to be one of these and it was none of them. So I could no longer hide behind my bizarre delusion. There were no aliens. There was no enemy but the one who hid inside me. Myself.

And yet—there was one fact which was not imaginary. Lois Worthington had died. She had seen the man in the back booth, I had tried to reach her, and she had been brutally murdered. This fact was all too real. And the vision I had so long ago of my father's death, that could not be dismissed or explained away now. That too had happened. At the time I was able to believe in coincidence. No longer.

Moreover, if the aliens existed only as part of an elaborate delusion of persecution, if whispered voices were halluccinations, there should have been accompanying symptoms before this, evidence of a greater deterioration of my thinking. But nothing else had changed. The world looked the same to me. I didn't even have to look far for a plausible explanation of my abrupt swings from apathy to extreme emotionalism. This instability could logically be accounted for by the unnatural pressures of fear and worry.

Dubiously I examined the evidence for and against the existence of the aliens. The structure of argument on which I could support belief in my sanity was weak, thin-walled, its foundations shallow. I closed my mind to shelter it against the winds of fact and logic.

I drove slowly away from the beach trailer community. There had been no sign of Laurie or Jenkins while I sat in the car. Some of the pain in my bruised body had subsided. Nothing after all had been broken except the tip of one tooth whose nerve throbbed like a hot wire in my jaw. My clothes were torn and bloody and the skin had been ripped off my knuckles, but otherwise I had come out of the fight in fair shape. The bruises would turn yellow and finally fade away, new skin would cover the knuckles, the puffiness around one eye would disappear, a plastic cap would disguise the broken tooth.

I glanced at the time dial on the instrument panel. It was not yet eleven o'clock. Still early. The forty-eight hours which had passed since the voices drew me across the campus toward the Dugout seemed more like endless weeks. Time had lost its meaning.

At this hour the shoreline road along which I moved was relatively deserted. Only an occasional car approached me along the outbound lanes. My pace was slow and one or two cars accelerated to pass me. The headlights of another slow-moving car bobbed in my rear view telescreen. Out on the causeway over the water traffic was much heavier, a glittering pattern of speeding lights.

A cat darted away from the side of the road. My foot jammed down in a sudden reflex action. I swerved sharply. For a second, the cat disappeared under the hood of the car and I felt a quick tension in expectation of the thump of contact. Then the cat reappeared, somehow having eluded the squealing tires, and I straightened the car. It had slowed almost to a crawl.

Accelerating, I glanced automatically into the rear view screen. The headlights of the car behind me were exactly the same distance away they had been before. For a moment I stared dully at the screen, not comprehending the significance of the other car's movement, yet aware that something was wrong. Understanding came slowly and, with it, the first bright streak of emotion to penetrate the gray cloud which enveloped me, a quick pulsation of fear.

I drove faster, climbing swiftly up from thirty to fifty miles an hour. The headlights remained steady on the screen, keeping pace. The car was following me.

There was a frozen moment when reality slipped away from me. I was aware of a creeping coldness, like the cutting chill of a damp wind, penetrating until my flesh crawled

87

and my teeth began to chatter uncontrollably. Somehow I kept the car on the road in its lane, maintaining the same speed. Then I saw the lights staring at me like eyes from the screen and I came out of my horrified trance with a jolt.

I had lost precious seconds. My foot jammed down and the little car leaped forward, the purr of its engine rising to a steady whine. The hills on my left side were a blur, and the clustered trailers on the ocean side of the road zipped past me with slapping wind sounds. I was approaching a speed of a hundred miles an hour and I had to fight to keep the light car on the road. It seemed to bounce and leap, hardly touching the ground.

And there were the headlights, dancing and winking on the small screen. The needle of the speedometer touched a hundred, edged past it—and at that instant I knew that I had played right into the pursuer's hands. This was what he wanted. This was to be the accident.

I slammed on the power brakes. They held, grinding loudly, while the car dipped and veered sharply, sliding into a skid.

"Release the brake!"

The thought cracked across my mind like the blow of a club. Momentarily stunned, I still kept my foot on the brake. The car was skidding dangerously now and the wheel seemed to have a life of its own, twisting and jumping in my hands. The scream of tires was like a cry of terror. But the car's speed had dropped swiftly.

"Release it!"

Sweat started on my forehead and under my arms. For a long moment my mind was locked in conflict with the force that tried to break it. Then, as if it were a wooden appendage attached to me but out of my control, my leg jerked. The car rolled free.

"Drive faster!"

I started to obey automatically as if the command had been my own, the message swiftly telegraphed from brain to foot. Anger brought resistance. I concentrated on steering the slowing car, trying to shut my mind, to create a blank wall of stubborn resistance. The muscles in my legs jerked with tension.

"Faster!" The word broke through like one of Jenkins' fists smashing through my feeble guard.

And, while my hands clenched the wheel until they ached, my foot inched inexorably toward the accelerator, nudged it, clamped down. The car lurched forward with gathering speed. A crushing weight of defeat made me slump on the seat. Tears of frustration blurred my vision of the road ahead. The speedometer climbed rapidly. A car's horn blasted and I swerved from the middle of the road back into my lane. I caught a glimpse of a red, angry face flashing past. The familiar headlights winked in the rear view screen like the eyes of the alien whose power had smashed through my flimsy barrier of resistance. Despair twisted like a fist in my stomach.

"Faster!" The voice that spoke in my mind was cold, unmoved, arrogant in its knowledge of power.

And I obeyed, letting myself relax, trying to ease the aching muscles of my arms and legs, not thinking about what I was going to do or what was about to happen to me. The speedometer's needle began to waver erratically above one hundred and ten miles an hour.

"Faster! Faster!"

The one word, repeated over and over, drumming in my brain until it obliterated thought. I was an automaton, steering the lurching, whining car along the blurred ribbon of road, a puppet controlled by tenuous strings of mental force, a wooden puppet without will or thought of its own, dumbly responding to the master's word.

And at last it came, the command, so dreaded in the deep recesses of my consciousness that protest shrieked in my mind, breaking me out of the stupor.

"Turn the wheel!"

And in that instant, when the immediate pull of obedience was almost overwhelming, a final frenzied cry of defiance was heard. I saw ahead the slanting curve of a ramp shooting out toward the ocean causeway. For long agonizing seconds I held out against the pressure—and when my hands moved on the wheel it was at that precise and last possible second which sent the car careening onto the ramp and into a long banked curve.

The maneuver caught my pursuer by surprise. There was a brief, bewildered respite before the clear cold voice spoke again, stamping out the elation that gripped me. The line of the causeway beckoned, so near now, less than a quarter of a mile away—

"Turn! Turn now!"

And I had spent the last remaining reserve of strength to resist. My hands obeyed. I spun the wheel.

The little car bounced off the low parapet at the edge of the ramp, kicked back out of control and shot across the narrow cement strip, its tail beginning a slow fishtailing motion, sliding into a spin. The low barrier on the other side of the ramp loomed up swiftly and I cringed against the impact—

And the car was caught by a sudden jerk that slammed me against the door with bone-jarring force. I felt the invisible electronic fingers of the automatic road controls grasping at the car, pulling it back, fighting against the momentum that carried it forward. Hope leaped in my chest. I had made it!

For a flashing second the car seemed to hang suspended, caught between the conflicting forces, and I was aware of the speeding lanes of traffic on the causeway now so near to me, of the whirling canopy of the star-stabbed sky, of the gray cold water surging far below. But the car's momentum had been too great. The plucking fingers of the electronic ribbon imbedded in the road slipped and lost their hold. The car's left front wheel and fender hit the parapet.

And the car was in mid-air, leaping the low wall and tumbling end over end in a long, soaring arc of flight, plummeting down, down, to smash at last into the wall of water. The wall broke and crashed around me and I plunged through it into a vast, unending pool of darkness.

15

FACES SWAM THROUGH the water, distorted and shimmering. There was a distant roaring in my ears like the clamor of the sea trapped in a seashell. The din faded away gradually and in the immensity of silence I waited shivering for the unseen force that would grip my mind.

"It's a miracle!" someone said clearly.

My eyelids pushed open like dusty blinds. I saw the faces again, blurred like a picture slightly out of focus but much sharper than before. I remembered an earlier awakening when five pairs of eyes had stared down at me in open curiosity and I had flinched in fear. Or had it all been a dream from which I was only now awakening?

"Don't move," a man said.

I had no intention of moving. My head ached and there was a deep throbbing in my arm, extending from a point near the shoulder down past the elbow, a throbbing not really painful but curiously electric and tingling.

I closed my eyes and re-opened them. There were two pairs of eyes, set in two faces which were quite clear. A man and a woman, middle-aged or older. Strangers. The man's hair was steel grey and very wet againt his skull. The woman looked like a bird. She bent toward me and I had the momentary impression that she was going to peck at me with her long, sharply-pointed nose.

"Can you hear us?" she asked in a thin, piping voice. "Do you know what we're saying?"

"Yes."

I thought I spoke aloud but she continued to watch me expectantly. Behind her the sky was black and the fact surprised me. I had somehow expected hot sunlight and a hard blue sky.

"Henry pulled you out of the car," the woman said. "We saw it happen."

I heard a breaker topple over and the swish-swish of two cars passing on the highway. Then I remembered.

"The voice!" I cried. "Turn the wheel!"

The man crouched over me threateningly. "What's that you said?"

I tried to twist away. Pain sliced through my head in a clean stroke that seemed to take the top of my skull off.

"Please!" I groaned. "The voice—"

"What about the voice?"

"It told me—turn—turn the wheel."

"Henry! Did you hear what he said?"

"He's delirious, mother. It don't mean anything."

"But he heard voices. He must be one of them."

"He doesn't know what he's saying."

My eyes had shut against the pain in my head. Opening them I saw the two people in sharply dimensional focus. The man was soaking wet. He appeared worried. The woman's bird-like features were curiously pinched, her eyes bright with excitement.

"Did you hear a voice?" she asked quickly. "Is that what you're trying to say? Did a voice speak to you?"

"Told me to turn," I said weakly. "The alien voice—"

"In your mind?" she demanded. "Can you hear voices—even when there aren't any people talking?"

I nodded faintly. "Tried to make me—kill myself."

"He needs a doctor," the man said suddenly.

"No!" The woman whirled on him. "The Exalted One would wish that he be brought to him."

"We aren't sure—"

"But he must be one who can hear the voices. You heard what he said—and you said yourself he should have been killed in that accident. If he hadn't been a Chosen One—"

"He might be hurt worse than we can see."

"The Swami will know. We must take him there."

Bewildered, I listened to them argue, not understanding what they could mean. They spoke in casual tones as if others had heard the voices. But if that were true then I was not alone, it wasn't something I had imagined—

"You've heard the voices?" I asked eagerly. "You've heard them?"

The brightness faded from her eyes, clouded over with sadness. She shook her head. "We try, Henry and me, but we can't hear them. We are weak. We have not learned the fullness of believing. But the Swami says we are approaching the purity of full knowledge." Her voice rose earnestly. "Our day will come—if not in this life, then in the next."

The man grunted, interrupting her. "Can you move your legs?" he asked of me.

I hesitated, then tried. I could wriggle my toes and flex my knees. I felt as if this were a great accomplishment.

The man shook his head. "You should have been killed," he said as if it were a grudging admission. "I guess maybe mother is right." He stood, turning toward the woman. "I'll bring the car down here. Don't let him move." He glanced down at me. "We can't do anything about your car right now. We'll report it and maybe they'll be able to fish it out. But the water's pretty deep there."

The loss of the car meant nothing to me. At the moment it did not even occur to me that the car was not mine and I would be responsible for any damage to it. The man had trudged up the beach toward the road and I stared at the bird woman.

"This person you're taking me to—has he heard them?"

"Oh, yes!" she said, evidently surprised. "He is exalted!"

I didn't understand. Fatigue pressed down on me and I was conscious of the pain in my head, of the deep throbbing in my arm. I tried to concentrate on what the couple had said, feeling an impatient excitement, but I couldn't seem to think clearly. I clung to the one fact that emerged clearly. There was someone else who had heard the voices, someone who could help me. I wouldn't be alone any more.

A car chugged through the soft sand and stopped nearby. A door opened. I felt hands sliding under my arms, lifting me. There was a cry of pain. A dizzying spiral of brightness whirled me around and around, released me, and I went sailing off into dark, empty space once more.

16

IT WAS MORNING when I woke. I felt stiff and sore, and for a minute I had the impression that I was encased from head to toe in thick white bandage. As I came more fully awake I realized that only my head and left arm were bandaged. I was dressed in a shapeless one-piece white gown that was tangled around my legs and torso.

I didn't know where I was. I lay in a hard, narrow bed between crisp, old-fashioned, white cotton sheets, the kind I had known as a child. The room was small and high-ceilinged. There was but one window, long and narrow and deeply inset with an elaborate metal grill. Though the window was curtainless, the wall was so thick that the rays of the sun were not direct but soft and filtered through the narrow aperture.

I pushed myself up, swinging my legs over the side of the bed. I had to brace myself as a dizzying wave of pain and nausea washed over me. I had the weak-limbed sensation of someone who has been in bed a long time. I wondered if I was in a hospital and how long I had been there.

There was a heavy carved wooden door at one end of the room with a small panel of opaque glass set into it at eye level. I had a fleeting impression that someone was watching me but I couldn't see through the glass.

Memory returned to me slowly in sharp-edged, broken fragments. I remembered being with Laurie, the fight with Jenkins outside her trailer, the headlong flight along the coast road, the lights staring at me from the rear view screen, the voice urging me to go faster and faster, and at last, the moment of terror when the car struck the parapet and tumbled through the air so fast that I was pinned against the seat.

And the couple who had loaded me into their car. They were taking me to see someone—

I heard a click. The door swung open and a small, sharp-featured woman trotted briskly into the room, clad in a loose white toga.

"You're awake!" she exclaimed.

The statement didn't seem to require an answer. I frowned at her.

"Don't you remember? We brought you here—Henry and I. The Swami was very pleased."

"Swami?"

"Yes! The Exalted One. He will see you this morning." She peered at me anxiously. "Are you feeling all right? The Swami said there was nothing broken. Your arm was badly cut and you had a concussion, that's all."

That was all. I felt as if I would never be able to move freely again. Yet I realized that I had once again been incredibly lucky. The alien had failed.

"Do you think you can eat?"

The thought of food brought back the acute sensation of nausea. I bent over, pressing one hand against my stomach, swallowing hard. I shook my head.

"You must have something," the woman said with a birdy peck of her head. "Don't try to walk yet."

She swept out, her toga trailing on the floor. The dust on the skirt marred the pristine white effect of the gown. I made no further attempt to move. The room swayed unsteadily around me whenever I stirred. I sat on the edge of the bed, unable to rouse myself to any real curiosity about where I was and why I had been brought here. Minutes ticked by and the woman did not return. The room was totally soundless. I could hear neither movement within it nor the sounds of a living world outside. Even the air conditioning was noiseless.

The place was like a crypt, I thought. The idea was peculiarly disturbing. I stared at the thick walls and the narrow slot of window and the heavy closed door, and they danced before my eyes as if they were edging forward, slowly closing in on me. A smothering claustrophobic fear clotted my throat and my breathing became labored and irregular.

Panic drove me off the bed. My clothes were laid neatly on a carved wooden chair against the wall. I staggered toward the chair. The floor of the room tilted and I had the sensation of falling, but somehow I reached the wall and leaned against it. After the room steadied, it took me several minutes to change from the white gown into my own coverall. I had to keep grabbing the chair for support. In spite of the cool temperature I was sweating.

Then I discovered that my shoes were missing. I looked very carefully around the room. There was no closet. The chair and the narrow bed were the only pieces of furniture. The floor itself was bare. My shoes weren't there.

I was still puzzling over this when the door opened and the bright-eyed bird woman tripped into the room carrying a tray. She stopped abruptly when she saw me.

"I told you not to get up," she said crossly.

I didn't answer her. She left the door open and I was staring at it. Air seemed to rush in through the opening. The smothering, closed-in feeling left me. How absurd, I thought. You're ill. You're imagining all kinds of dangers.

"You'd better sit on the bed," the woman said. "Can you make it? I guess you can, getting dressed and all."

I went obediently to the bed. It was easier this time. Even the dizziness was subsiding. I could smell the fragrance of hot tea. On the tray there were also some dry crackers and a bowl of some kind of dried meal that looked like rice but was hard and crunchy like a seed. To my own surprise the sight of the food made me hungry.

I ate. The meal was tasteless but not unpleasant. The crackers and the tea were excellent. I seemed to feel strength pouring into me as I ate. By the time I had finished I felt almost normal.

I glanced up at the woman, who sat perched on the edge of the chair with a bright-eyed air of interest. She even cocked her head and peered at me sideways like a bird. She wore a thin little smile.

"Where are my shoes?" I asked suddenly.

She was startled. "Oh, we never wear shoes here!"

And for the first time I saw that her feet were bare. No wonder she moved so silently. I thought of hundreds of people padding throughout the building on silent, naked feet. The idea was more comical than frightening.

"And where is here?" I asked.

Her tone was lower, almost reverent. "You are in the Temple of the Western Sun," she said. "You have been granted an audience with the Exalted One. He has already seen you and laid his hand upon you."

I frowned. Phrases came back to me from the previous night, and from somewhere came an image of a very brown man with luminous black eyes staring at me, bending close. And I remembered why I had been brought here. I looked sharply at the woman. Her husband had saved my life. And they had said something about the alien voices.

"I owe you my life," I said. "Your husband pulled me out of the car."

She smiled. "We saw it happen. Henry swam out and got you. Then when you said you had heard a voice, that an evil voice had forced you to turn off the road—"

"There's someone else here who has heard the voices?" I asked eagerly. "You said—"

"The Exalted One hears," she said calmly. "It's strange that you should have heard them when so many of us have tried so hard and failed. But the waters of God's purpose are deep and hard to fathom."

The last words dropped incongruously from the woman's lips, spoken with a kind of mechanical precision that was very familiar to me: the recitation by rote of an approved answer by a student who does not understand. The curiosity growing in me was checked by some misgivings. I was eager to meet the man she called the Exalted One. I had heard of mystical religious cults, of course—their numbers had grown rapidly in recent years—and it was probable that I had stumbled upon one of these. But I grasped at the straw of fact that was offered to me: the man had

97

heard bodiless voices. However he might have interpreted them, wasn't it possible that he might have heard the aliens?

"When can I see him? I'd like to talk to him now."

"He is in contemplation," the woman said. "But it won't be long now." She nodded toward the window, through which one could perceive only a sliver of blue sky. "When the sun is overhead he will call you."

Her expression became grave. "You will want to prepare yourself. I will come for you then."

Before I could stop her, she bustled out, her naked feet making almost inaudible slaps on the bare tile floor.

She came for me at noon. I had dozed and woke refreshed. My arm was painful when I moved it, but my head was clearer and my vision sharp. The woman led me along a wide arched corridor with a great number of doors similar to the one to my room. We came out onto a balcony. Stairs led down into a high-ceilinged lobby. To my surprise, the huge room was almost empty. One white-robed figure hurried out of sight. The place as silent as my room had been. Here, however, sunlight streamed through a huge triangle of stained glass, splashing a pool of many colors across the tile floor and the bare white walls.

We walked across the lobby and through another door. Here I stopped abruptly. The room was crowded, all of the people wearing white togas like the woman wore. They were all sitting cross-legged on the floor in various attitudes of concentration. Many did not even look up as I entered. Those who did showed neither surprise nor particular interest. They went back to their contemplations. No one spoke.

The woman had crossed the room. Now she beckoned me forward impatiently. I walked slowly toward her. She opened the door at the end of the room and stepped aside to let me pass. I heard the door shut gently behind me.

At first I thought I was alone. The room was heavily curtained and very dark. There was a strong smell of incense. The room seemed bare except for a single cushion in the center. Then I realized that a thin, filmy curtain hung like a veil across the room. Behind it a light began to glow, starting at the bottom corners of the room and brightening gradually like a sunrise. Behind the veil, thrown into relief by the soft glow of blue light behind him, was an almost naked man. He wore a thick white turban wrapped around his head. In the center of the crown was set a fiery red stone. The man's features were touched only with highlights—a straight line defining a strongly-bridged nose, other strokes suggesting high cheek-bones, sensuously full lips, a firm jawline—creating the overall impression of a face that was startlingly handsome without being weak or pretty. The skin of his body looked almost black. A slash of white cloth covered his loins.

"You are Paul Cameron," the man said, an impressively rich and resonant voice lending importance to the statement.

"That's right." It was disconcerting to hear my own voice, thin and colorless in contrast.

"The cushion has been provided for you," he said. "You are not accustomed to our more austere habits."

The tone was faintly deprecating, suggested a softness and civilized weakness in me for which I couldn't be blamed. I sat on the cushion with a feeling of defiance. When I was seated on the floor I found that I had to look up toward the man and I realized that he sat on a raised platform. It occurred to me that the relative positions were carefully calculated.

"I must thank you for treating me," I said, feeling vaguely disappointed. I don't know what I had expected but it was not this elaborately staged piece of theater. I was rapidly concluding that I was simply in the temple of one of those popular and phony cults that dupe the credulous.

The man bowed his head. "I am Swami Fallaninda. You are disappointed?"

His perception of my thought surprised me. "No, not at all. You know how I came here."

99

"Your emanations are strong," he said, his voice booming at me resonantly. "I feel the vibrations. . . ."

In spite of myself I felt a tug of hope. "When I spoke of hearing voices your—disciples became excited. Have you heard them?"

"Many hear. The astral body is visible to those who can tune in its vibrations, who can see and hear with astral eyes and ears."

I broke in impatiently. "These aren't astral voices or whatever you call them. These are aliens. They tried to kill me!"

The mystic showed neither surprise nor concern. "It is possible that occult powers can be used for evil purposes. Yet it is not usual for this to be so, nor is it usual for one to be consciously receptive to the vibrations of higher frequency given by even a powerful adept, learned in the control of the mind, unless the listener has been trained in the development of astral vision. You have had no such training."

"No—but I've heard voices!"

"Perhaps it would be better if you would explain what you have experienced."

For a moment I studied the dark figure half-hidden behind the veil. Inexplicably, my first doubts and suspicions had begun to slip away from me. The man inspired confidence. I had forgotten the theatrical trappings of the setting as the rich voice filled the room—gentle, soothing, inviting belief and faith and trust. I found the hope growing in me. He had not, after all, dismissed my claim to hear the voices in my mind. He acted as if the fact was not at all unusual.

I told him the story. I saw little reason to conceal anything. Beginning with my memory of the vision of my father's death, I went on to recount the more recent vivid dream of drowning and the many times I had heard the voices, particularly in recent weeks they had come to me with increasing clarity and frequency. And finally, I spoke of the two attempts of my life when an alien force had seemed to control my mind. When I had finished, I waited anxiously, peering through the thin fabric of the veil.

"I have known it," the swami said suddenly in his incredibly deep baritone. "The evil vibrations have reached me, but I resisted the truth which they would have led me to believe." He bowed his head. "Thus have I failed to keep contact with the Universal Mind."

"The Universal Mind?" I repeated.

"The Cosmic Consciousness toward which we grope. The human mind is frail and finite, but the Universal Mind is all."

"I don't understand."

I thought he sighed. "All human life is a groping upwards, an opening of the individual mind to the One Universal Mind. Our consciousness is limited. We catch only fragmentary glimpses of the truth, the great body of superconsciousness which lies on another plane, through which we must move closer to God, the One Universal Mind. But the history of man is a story of this struggle upward toward the light, the slow evolution of consciousness toward that state when at last the subconscious and the superconscious will be merged in the One, and the One in all."

"What does that have to do with me?" I demanded.

"There have been men, advanced members of the human race, who have attained to Cosmic Consciousness, the state of true wisdom. Even in ancient times these have lived—the Yogi of India, the Magus of Persia, the Atlantean Kushog—"

"So I've heard," I snapped irritably. "But I'm not interested in ancient mystics—"

He held up his hand in a commanding gesture. His voice rose, vibrant and dominating. "Listen! Do not close your mind to the truth of the ancients! For they have lived, they live now, whom you do not comprehend, who have discovered the wisdom of the East, who know that there is no pain, no sickness, no evil beyond the power of the mind to control. All men may approach this realm if they but wish it. It is necessary to purify the self, to rise above the

101

interfering vibrations of material need and base emotions and ego-dominated thoughts, to learn control of the body and the mind. Only then can we rise like the phoenix from the ashes of a dead ego, into a new life in the higher plane where the self does not exist."

The rich voice thundered through the room, swelling and resounding from the walls, and suddenly sank to a bare whisper. I found myself leaning forward, straining to hear.

"Telepathy is but a simple tool of the adept who has learned control of the mind of man. Such a one can easily communicate directly with the unconscious mind of another, can cause a weaker mind to do its bidding—can even cause the strange delusions which you have described. Such is the power of the Cosmic Consciousness! And such power, used for evil, can only be defeated by a true inner faith, an attainment of purity in which all base emotions are cleansed. Yours is a unique gift, a reflection of the Cosmic Power you have known in a previous incarnation. To use this power of the mind, you must learn that total concentration in which there is no sensation, no awareness of self. You must be an empty receptacle, ready to be filled with wine of truth and love."

Incredulous, I stared at the shadowy figure under his white turban. While he had spoken, the apparent majesty of his words and the magnetic power of his voice had held me. For a moment, I had felt a thrill of understanding and belief. Here was the answer to everything! Here was the end of fear and wonder! But now, in the sudden silence, I heard the echo of his vibrant phrases, glib and full of half-truths, promising much and saying little. All he offered were vague speculations about someone using occult powers against me, speculations mixed up with a hodge-podge of Hindu and Oriental teachings blended into a palatable opiate.

And all at once, I thought of the acoustics of this room and I understood why my own voice, swallowed up by the sponge-like walls surrounding my half of the room, had seemed so weak and helpless, while his, obviously reinforced by a clever acoustical arrangement and possibly even by microphones, boomed at me with stereophonic richness.

Angrily I jumped to my feet. "What are you suggesting? Do you want me to join your little camp of followers? How about my life savings? I won't need that, will I, if I'm going to purify myself of all earthly desires?"

His voice was heavy and sad. "You have closed your mind. It was to be expected. You are not ready to believe."

"I'm certainly not ready to swallow that stuff about someone using cosmic powers against me. Who is it? Why should he try to kill me? Maybe you could go into a trance and communicate with him for me. I'd like a few more answers."

My anger was out of proportion, but I couldn't control it. Disappointment was so keen that it severed any bonds of restraint. I had placed too much hope on the help I might find here. To encounter a dedicated fanatic—or what was worse, a clever charlatan—enraged me. I stepped forward and tore at the veil which hung between us. The fabric gave off a faint smell of dust disturbed and a weak spot ripped under my hand.

The swami did not move.

"Answer me, damnit! Who's trying to kill me? Or am I as crazy as you are!"

He remained absolutely still, head bent, legs folded under him, his attitude one of total concentration—or prayer. Furious, I grabbed his shoulders and jerked him up. His lack of weight astonished me. The man was thin and bony, fragile and light under my hands. The large, handsome head was an incongruity on the short, frail body. No wonder he sat on a platform! No wonder he spoke out of darkness! I stared into the black, liquid eyes. His lack of resistance finally penetrated through the angry haze of frustration which had filmed my reason. I released him.

I hadn't heard any sound behind me. I caught the blur of a white robe swooping over me and heard too late the padding of many feet. Then I was enveloped in a smothering white blanket that dropped over my head. Hands caught and pinned my arms and dragged me down, hauling me backwards—

"Wait!"

The swami's voice thundered its command and the room was stilled. I was on the floor, held there by the weight of a heavy body and the pressure of many grasping hands. There was an angry mutter of protest.

"Release him!"

Reluctantly, the hands drew away. Someone pulled the white cloth off me. I blinked up at a huddle of white-robed figures looking down at me, their eyes hostile. I recognized among the faces that of Henry, the man who had saved my life.

"Evil has touched him," the swami said. The men standing over me drew back as if in fear. "Let him go in peace."

Warily I pushed myself up. The others made no attempt to stop me now. They were all watching the Exalted One. He was standing now, and even on the raised platform he made a small, unimpressive figure when erect. But there was nothing pale or thin about the cultivated voice.

"The days of the spirit are at hand," he intoned. "The hours of evil are numbered. Go in peace. Cleanse your spirit! Prepare for the day of Truth, of the All-in-One. You, who have stumbled blindly upon the latent powers that lie within, know that when your mind is opened to truth the powers or darkness can hold no influence over you. Know your own strength, believe in it—fear not to die! For there is no death; there is only the life of the spirit."

To my astonishment, those who had a moment before been violently tearing at my body now sank slowly, one by one, to the floor, ignoring my presence. Only the swami himself still watched me. The red glow of the gem in his turban was like a fiery eye. Uneasily, I stumbled back through the motionless heaps of white-shrouded figures kneeling or sitting on the floor. The door was open. I turned and ran.

In the lobby I was abruptly confronted by the bird-faced woman. Her features were pinched tight, her eyes bright with venom.

"We should have left you to die!" she screeched. "You put your hands on the swami!"

"There is no death," I muttered.

I left her open-mouthed. A moment later, I burst out of the cool lobby into the bright, hot sunlight. I was striding swiftly away from the temple before I realized that I was still barefooted.

I turned to look back at the Temple of the Western Sun, an architectural anachronism that, like the swami's faith, dated back to a time lost in the reaches of history. The sunlight reflected glaringly from the arched roof and from the intricate pattern of color in the big stained glass window at the front.

I was intensely relieved to be out of the place into the open air. Here I could breathe freely, free of the dusty heritage of an ancient wisdom founded on love and the aspiration of man to be one with the source of all things, the Creator of the universe, a wisdom now half-absorbed and clouded by a ritual of words. And I felt ashamed of my relief. The small satisfaction derived from my final taunt to the bird woman crumbled before the knowledge that I had bolted from the temple in foolish panic. I would have come to no harm at the swami's hands. In the end he had acted far better than I. Perhaps he was not a charlatan. One couldn't blame him for using a few dramatic effects to heighten the impact of his message. What religion had not? And his last words had had a ring of sincerity. He believed. It was I who, driven by blind anger, had almost been guilty of violence, because the man had failed me. And yet—

Standing there, staring at the silent temple, I had the obscure feeling that he had said something that was very important to me, something I could not quite grasp, a truth buried under the avalanche of his words.

17

I ARRIVED AT my trailer in the middle of the afternoon. My feet were tired and blistered, although I had managed to pick up a pair of sandals along the way. The swami's temple had been a good mile from the nearest elevated station. I wasn't used to that much walking, particularly in my bare feet.

Just as I turned into the walk leading up to my trailer, the girl next door appeared. She ran down the steps toward me and halted abruptly. For a change her eyes were not cast down or averted but intent on my face, wide with concern. I had a startlingly clear sense of her anxiety, followed by an apprehension of acute relief.

"You're—you're all right?" she asked breathlessly.

She was staring at the bandage around my head. My coverall concealed the larger bandage extending from my left shoulder to the elbow.

"Banged up a little," I said with forced cheerfulness. "Nothing serious."

"I was afraid—" She caught herself. "When you didn't return home, I—"

I looked at her sharply and she blushed. Her head turned away quickly, but not before I saw the creeping stain of red under her skin. For a moment, I was too astonished to reply. The girl's next words made me forget all about her odd behavior.

"The police were here," she said, her glance brushing mine for only an instant. "They wished to see you."

I felt a quick stab of warning. My gaze narrowed, trying to read her expression. The police had not been satisfied with my story, then. And this girl had backed up my alibi.

"Were they questioning you again—about the other night?" I asked with an attempt at casualness.

"Oh, no!" She shook her head in a terse, firm negative.

"They were very nice. They said they would stop back to see you later."

"You didn't—tell them anything else?"

A faint smile touched her lips and I seemed to see her face revealed for the first time without the mask of shyness. It was a face that mirrored warmth and a hidden humor, a sensitive, lovely face.

"There was no need," she said. "I do not think they are interested any more."

"But they didn't say why they wanted to see me?"

All at once she appeared to become aware of my close scrutiny and she took a step back. "Nothing," she said quickly. "They—they told me nothing."

She started to turn away and I stepped quickly toward her, catching her arm. "Wait!" I said urgently. I could feel a faint trembling under my fingers, a current of— what? Excitement? Fear? "I want to thank you—for being worried about me."

Her eyes met mine briefly and I was surprised to see that they reflected none of the timidity or apprehension that seemed to vibrate in her body.

"It is only natural that I would be concerned," she said, and even her voice held a different tone, a note of surprising tenderness.

And while I stared, she pulled away from me and ran lightly up the steps and into her trailer. The door closed firmly behind her.

I took a step after her. Her words came back to me, her news about the police. They would be back. And there could be only one reason for their wanting to talk to me again.

It took all the control I had to keep from turning and running.

I let myself into my trailer. It seemed stuffy inside, the clean, cool, filtered air slightly stale after a day without human smells to combat. An impulse of caution made me go through the trailer quietly. In the compact, carefully planned rooms, it would have been impossible for anyone to hide. I felt the absurdity of expecting to find police lurking in the closet or under the bed, but I was not acting very rationally. The desire to flee followed me through the empty rooms.

A woman had been killed and the police had reason to think that I might be involved. And I had lied. Why else should I lie unless I was guilty? From their point of view the conclusion was obvious. And then it occurred to me that they might have even more reason than I knew to find me a prime suspect. Evidence could have been planted to incriminate me. Why not? It would be one way to muffle the listener's ears. Modern forces of justice were quick and unsentimentally ruthless in dealing with a murderer. They had to be in an overcrowded world.

Restraint snapped. I ran into the bedroom and fumbled hastily in the closet for my one small suitcase. Tossing it onto the bed, I began to pull a few clothes out of the closet and the chest. I snatched a razor from the washstand and a windproof jacket from its hook. When I had jammed everything into it and slammed it shut, I stood over the suitcase, panting. It seemed to me that I could smell my own fear, sharp and acrid, soiling the conditioned air. I felt an unexpected revulsion.

I sat on the bed. For a long moment I didn't move. My mind seemed frozen. The trailer was very silent and I listened to my own strained breathing. And at last I held up my fear and examined it, and I knew that I could not run.

I was not guilty. Flight, in any event, would be more incriminating than anything I could possibly do, and if they were really after me I would be picked up within hours.

Besides, I thought without humor, I could always plead insanity.

I had less than an hour to wait. I heard the helicopter whirring overhead and was at the window when it dropped gently onto the landing strip across the street. The two policemen came directly toward my trailer, moving unhurriedly. I recognized the chunky sergeant who had questioned me before. The same lean partner was with him. I opened the door as they reached the steps.

Sgt. Bullock looked up mildly. "Glad we caught you in, Mr. Cameron."

"I heard you were looking for me."

"Yeah, we thought you might be a little worried about the case we talked to you about."

I stared at him, puzzled. His attitude was not that of the aggressive policeman. He seemed almost apologetic.

"We have our job to do, Mr. Cameron, and we have to run down every possibility just as a matter of routine."

"Sure. I understand."

He grinned. The square face which had appeared so mean and hard acquired the pudgy friendliness of a well-fed puppy.

"You have to admit it looked kind of funny, your asking about the girl and her being killed a couple of hours later. It's the kind of thing we can't ignore."

"Yes, of course. Have you—discovered anything new? I mean, do you know who did it?"

"Oh, yeah, we got him. The owner of the restaurant where she worked."

"Harry?"

"That's his name. Seems like he's been crazy about the girl and there's been a little trouble before. She was the friendly type. I guess she's been servicing half the college crowd."

I shook my head. "Harry," I repeated blankly.

"Yeah. Well, he's caused trouble before this when he caught her with some kid. He hangs around her place and he beat her up a couple of times. So it looks like he was jealous and they had a battle and he lost his head." The sergeant shrugged. "Happens every day."

Still stunned, I stared at the two officers. The full implications of what Sgt. Bullock had said were just beginning to penetrate. If Harry was the killer—

"Are you sure?" I asked.

The sergeant appeared surprised. "Oh, he hasn't confessed yet. We picked him up a few hours ago and he wouldn't say anything. Stubborn guy. But we'll have the results of the lie detector and serum tests within a few hours and that'll wrap it up. He did it, all right. He was seen near her place that night, and the neighbors heard them quarreling. We'll be digging up more stuff on him, now that we got it pinned down."

I felt a numbing cold settling at the base of my neck. "Thanks for taking the trouble to tell me this," I said thickly.

"No trouble, Mr. Cameron. This is our patrol area anyway. We're around here pretty regular. Just thought we'd drop by and take a load off your mind."

"Thanks."

The thin, silent partner spoke for the first time. "Never thought you did it anyway," he said laconically.

I tried a smile. My lips felt like stiff rubber. "You had me worried. I'm glad it's all cleared up."

"Yeah," the sergeant said heavily. "So are we."

They turned away. I managed to utter a reply to their casual goodbyes. They crossed the street and climbed into the helicopter. A moment later, it rose slowly into the air. I watched it until it had dwindled out of sight, lost in the afternoon haze.

All over, I thought. The mystery all cleared up. No mystery at all. There never had been one. Lois Worthington's murder had been the one tangible proof I had that the aliens were real and dangerous. But she had been killed by a jealous lover.

There were no more threads to cling to.

I stumbled back into the trailer. Dropping onto the couch under the long window, I lay motionless, my eyes open and unseeing, fixed on some distant point beyond the ceiling. My mind turned over sluggishly. With careful logic I tried to examine all the facts. Like a policeman, I thought, investigating a crime. A reported crime. You check each

110

suspect, eliminating them one by one. When the list is limited that's not hard. I had done that. None of my four suspects was capable of the monstrous plot I had imagined. None had superhuman powers. So there were no suspects. Better take another look at the crime, a close look. Question the witnesses, see if their testimony is reliable, make sure it stands up. This time there was only one witness who claimed that a crime had been committed, an attempt at murder. The victim himself, Paul Cameron. Queer duck, a bastard, mother's dead so he lives alone, keeps pretty much to himself, no close friends. Got a vivid imagination. Keeps hearing things. Is he the only witness to the fact that there was a crime? Yes. Well, how do we know he's not lying? How do we know it's not all in his mind?

And that was it. Investigation completed. There was no crime. There were no aliens.

For long, painful, unaccounted minutes I confronted this inevitable conclusion. Then, in one of those odd mental leaps that seem to have no apparent motive, like the sudden sideways jump of a grasshopper, I thought of Swami Fallaninda, the Exalted One. I could hear the vibrant echo of his voice. "Know that when your mind is opened to truth the powers of darkness can hold no influence over you." A wise platitude, I thought. When you examined with the cold objectivity of distance any of the little man's pompous phrases, they resolved themselves into very ordinary statements. His devoted circle of followers thought he was a man apart, a special being in touch with the Cosmic Consciousness, a man one with God. The brief episode with the little mystic had left an unusually deep impression on me —but the message he brought back from his astral plane could not save me.

There was another god left to me, one I had not turned to, the last one who stood between me and the powers of darkness which sought to possess my mind—the man of science.

18

DR. JONAS TEMPLE was a man of about sixty, whose appearance belied his years. His hair was a crisp iron gray, cropped close to a large, strongly-modeled head. His features were heavy without being coarse and the flesh was firm and ruddy. Of medium height and powerfully built, he looked more like an athletically vigorous man who was capable of exhausting physical labor than a renowned geophysicist who seldom left the pale blue atmosphere of his laboratory.

His eyes, bright blue and intelligent, regarded me steadily. Their expression was thoughtful and appraising rather than mocking. I felt grateful.

I knew that I had been fortunate in finding him in his office alone on a Saturday evening. The building was almost empty. One of Dr Temple's assistants was working in a small laboratory down the hall and janitors were puttering about the building on their routine cleanup chores. I reflected that it was an index to the character of the man in front of me that I would have found him here, still working at the end of a long day, tireless and dedicated. And it was even more characteristic that he would take the time to listen to my story without laughing or showing impatience.

"Let's review what you're suggesting," Dr. Temple said. He touched a jet of flame to the fragrant ash in the deep bowl of his pipe. "What you're asking me to believe is that some form of alien life has assumed human form—"

"Possessed human bodies."

"Ah, yes. Possessed." The blue eyes squinted at me speculatively, and I knew that the word had called to mind the devil-possessions and exorcisms which had once been so prominent a part of the history of Christianity. "They

112

control these bodies as their own. A kind—intelligent parasite."

I nodded. I could feel the tension in my body as I waited, like a network of wires being stretched tighter.

"And you can hear their thoughts?" Dr. Temple asked. "They're telepaths."

"But that means you are, too, because you're the only one who hears them."

"Yes," I said stubbornly.

"Can you hear mine? Can you project yours to me?"

I was silent. This was one of the barriers I had run into every time I reviewed the facts in my mind. There was one answer I had tried to accept, but even as I voiced it now I knew it didn't sound convincing.

"Perhaps true telepathy—direct and conscious tele-communication as opposed to the random reception of a thought —requires two beings capable of extra sensory perception in a highly developed degree—sender and receiver."

"Which would help to explain why this—this talent of yours hasn't revealed itself before now.

"But it has! That is, there were things like the vision of my father's death—not telepathy but related experience, clairvoyance. "

"Yes." The scientist frowned. "You will forgive me, Mr. Cameron, if I do not give too much weight to that experience. It's not at all uncommon. People envision harm to those close to them every day and it is inevitable that they will think it extraordinary when one day something does happen."

"But I didn't even know my father existed!"

"Perhaps." The voice was gentle, the blue eyes kindly. "You could easily have known that he did, by deduction or through some chance remark of your mother's. You could have reached the conclusion subconsciously while not admitting it on a conscious level because you found the fact unpleasant to face."

"That's possible," I said slowly, unconvinced.

"Mr. Cameron, I'm not trying to ridicule what you have

113

suggested. I am just trying to review all the implications of what you're asking for me to believe—asking yourself to believe—and we must restrict ourselves to directly pertinent information. Your vision of your father's death could or could not be relevant. There are, I admit, fairly well authenticated cases of clairvoyance. But with reference to your recent experiences, that earlier vision is inconclusive and subject to varying interpretations."

He shifted in his chair and sucked vigorously at his pipe until the bowl glowed red. As I waited in the stillness of his office for him to continue, my eyes strayed past him to the cabinets along one entire wall. Behind glass doors was the famous collection of Martian crystal and fossil formations, to the study of which the scientist had devoted his life. Surely these must have revealed something of the nature of Martian life. If some kind of intelligent parasite had existed there, wouldn't it leave traces detectible to a man like Temple?

"This alien form of life you postulate could exist," Dr. Temple said. "Grant that. There is no reason why life, intelligent life, on other planets would have to be recognizable to us. What you postulate is essentially a form of parasite, and the idea of a parasitical being which is also intelligent is not completely beyond the evidence of life we know even on earth. Let us concede that it could happen. An intelligent being, evolving under vastly different environmental conditions, might discover early in the progress of evolution that it could use a material host with a more highly developed physical organism but an undeveloped intelligence. And through the eons of change and self-improvement such an intelligent being might evolve physically only along those lines which would be necessary to its survival and its mental development. If it could use the body of a host, it would tend not to improve its own self-sufficient physical organism, as man has developed his body, but rather to perfect the ability to seize and to control its varied hosts."

114

I nodded eagerly, feeling hope stir and unfold. It was possible!

"However," the scientist said slowly, "it's rather a difficult step to accept the idea that such a parasitical life form could live in *any* host—even one from another planet and with a totally strange organism, such as man."

"But it is conceivable," I said doggedly, unable to relinquish the blossoming hope.

"Perhaps. We know so little of life, of the living organism. We know, or at least we think we know, that any highly developed being would have cells, and that it would be constructed ultimately of the same limited number of atoms from which everything in our universe is manufactured. But the forms which life could take are infinite. And the possibility which you suggest has one interesting facet." He paused and I leaned forward, feeling sweat on my palms. "An intelligent parasite," Dr. Temple said thoughtfully, "controlling and living within its host, feeding upon its host or upon what the host consumed, is one form of life which could easily survive space travel— providing its host could survive. For the parasite's own environment within the host would not substantially be altered."

He glanced at me sharply, as if a sudden thought had occurred to him. "But why wouldn't such an intelligent being, its mental capacities presumably far beyond man's if your experience is any indication, have mastered space travel long before us? Why should it be dependent upon an inferior intelligence?"

"Because it didn't have a host like man to use," I said quickly. "That seems to be one main reason for coming here—and for wanting to bring other aliens here. They've never known a physical organism like man. They haven't developed one themselves because they didn't need to—or possibly because it wouldn't have been able to exist under Martian conditions of life. Their hosts never developed the perfection of usefulness man's body has reached with his arms and hands and fingers. What's more, we know that Mars is almost a dead planet. Wouldn't a parasite eagerly seize upon any new organism that came along—especially one that was physically far superior to anything that had evolved on Mars?"

Dr. Temple nodded slowly. "Yes, that is a plausible explanation." He sighed. "It's all possible, Mr. Cameron, all plausible—up to a point. The existence of extra sensory powers in such an intelligence would be quite natural—even inevitable. But—"

There was reluctance in his voice, compassion in his eyes. "Go on," I said harshly.

"There are two objections to your theory for which I can find no answer. One is that my own studies do not reveal any evidence of the kind of creature you have postulated. And I am led irrevocably to the conclusion that there would be tell-tale signs."

"And the other?" I whispered.

"The second objection is the manner in which this parasite actually came to earth—on a returning space ship. This we have from the aliens, themselves, according to what you overheard. This is the only way they could have got to earth. And yet that way is impossible."

I didn't want to ask why. The word was thick and hard and painful in my throat but I had to voice it. "Why? Why?"

"Your alien said something about transfering to another body—and you concluded that he meant this was necessary for the return trip through space to Mars. What is especially pertinent, he wanted to effect this transfer at the last possible moment when it would be too late for any close physical examination."

"Yes, one of them said something like that."

"And obviously, Mr. Cameron, we do not need the alien to give us the information that they would want to avoid close examination of the host. The presence of a powerful parasitical organism in man's body can quite readily be detected. We might not know what it was but we would know that it was there. We must assume that this would

116

be particularly true in the case of a parasite so powerful that it was able to control directly the human body and mind. Any exhaustive examination would reveal the alien's existence in the body."

I felt the hope withering, turning brown and fragile.

"Mr. Cameron," Dr. Temple said quietly, "no parasite entered earth in the body of any of the men who came back. I need hardly tell you that each of those men was put through exhaustive, painstakingly complete physical and mental tests under rigidly controlled conditions, even before coming in contact with any humans back here on earth. You see, we had to be careful. There was the risk of bringing back deadly viruses that might not yet have visibly affected the men. There was the question of radiation, of contagious diseases, of any number of harmful effects. In addition, the very fact that these men had survived extensive space flight made them priceless subjects for study. Mr. Cameron, you needn't take my word for it, you can easily verify what I'm saying, but nothing unusual could have escaped the examination these men underwent." Dr. Temple swung toward the glass cases along the wall. "Why, even every bit of rock and bone and dead fungus you see in these cabinets was exhaustively examined and re-examined and tested with every means known to science before ever being touched by human hands!"

"But there must be some way—"

"Let me finish. There is another factor which you may have failed to consider, one that you could not be expected to know. The men on our ship never once came in direct physical contact with any object on Mars or among the items brought back from that planet. The landing party was never directly exposed even to the Martian atmosphere. It was too great a risk. A protective wall always interposed between the men and the objects they contacted. Nothing was touched by human hands. So how would a parasite have made entry?"

"I don't know!" I said harshly. "But it happened!"

Something stirred in my mind, something urged into

117

activity by Dr. Temple's words, but the moment I concentrated on it, trying to isolate it, a door seemed to close solidly down a dimly lighted corridor of my mind.

"Maybe it was dormant when it was brought in," I said desperately. "Maybe it didn't show up under the tests. How can we be so sure our instruments tell us everything?"

For a moment the scientist did not answer. I saw the compassion in his eyes and knew that he did not believe the aliens existed. He was trying to be kind and patient. I was taking up a great deal of his valuable time but he gave no indication of this. His pipe had burnt out again and now he set it carefully in the big ash tray on his desk. He leaned forward.

"Mr. Cameron, I am a scientist. When I'm presented with a strange new set of facts or apparent facts, even if they seem to contradict my own established theories, I have to consider them. I must try to let the facts speak for themselves without my imposing a preconceived meaning upon them. I've tried not to do that with what you've told me. I've tried to consider seriously the theory or explanation you've offered for the particular set of facts. However, when investigation appears to preclude one possible explanation we have to look for another, an alternative meaning, and see if it will provide a vessel into which the facts might fit precisely. In the present situation there does seem to be another possible answer."

"I know what you're going to say—"

"There may be no alien minds," Dr. Temple said quietly. "Or rather, there may be only one. Your own."

The words dropped with a brutal finality into my brain.

"I am not a psychiatrist," Dr. Temple went on gently, each word falling like the blow of a hammer, "but everything you have told me admits of a known delusional pattern with which even I am familiar. The presence of enemies with superhuman powers, your own possession of abnormal abilities and the fact that your unique talents make you an object of persecution by these enemies, seems to fit a schizophrenic syndrome. I would have to look it up, but—"

"That won't be necessary," I said dully. "I looked it up. Paranoid schizophrenia."

"The hallucinations, if I'm not mistaken, both visual and auditory are also part of that pattern," the scientist added. "And also the indications of withdrawal which you've admitted. Even the idea of being possessed, forced to do things you don't want to—"

"Oh, yes," I agreed bitterly. "It all fits. Perfectly."

Dr. Temple caught himself and stopped abruptly, as if embarrassed by his own absorption in the problem. He coughed self-consciously. I avoided his eyes. Silence was loud in the room.

"I'm sorry, Mr. Cameron," the scientist said at last. "You have come to me for help. I can't give it to you— but I think you can help yourself. You were confronted suddenly when you were young with a shocking fact which apparently destroyed your sense of security. Now, years later, your attempt to escape the reality you tried to push out of your mind has created an intolerable conflict. But now that you know what has happened you can resolve that conflict. You can face the reality. After all, it is not so very important or shameful to know that you are the bastard son of a very distinguished scientist and a woman you loved deeply. Is it so hard to accept that you must escape from it into fantasy?"

I shook my head, unable to answer. The mind is not that simple, I thought. It does not move in such neatly laid out channels. I rose stiffly and walked to the windows. For a moment I stood there staring at the city becoming lost in darkness. On impulse, I opened one window. Fresh, cool air washed against my face. I stood listening to the whisper of voices, soft in the distance, to the tinkling fall of laughter.

The final god had spoken. I knew at last, without doubt, that I was insane.

19

ALONE AND ON foot, I wandered through the garish streets of the city. I moved without purpose or destination, with the drunk's uncertain and aimless step. Like the sponge it resembled, my brain soaked up the sights and sounds, soon became sodden with the glut of sensation until the images were overlapping, blurred and meaningless. I walked. Around me there was the blare of horns, the swish of tires on pavement, the scrape and clip of feet along the sidewalk, the eager call and the murmured phrase. Overhead, the slow and heavy throbbing of a helicopter or, higher in distance and frequency, the whine and clap of a jet slapping through the sound barrier. Sometimes the rumble of an unseen train speeding along the monorail nearby, whistling shrilly as it neared a stop. At intervals the clashing sound effects and throbbing voices from a public telescreen, rising in volume and urgency as I approached, then fading slowly behind me. And always there was music, blaring from a loudspeaker, muffled by an intervening wall, exploding as a door was opened. The soar of a violin, the call of a trumpet, the crash of a drum, the croon of a human voice. All these followed me along the crowded streets.

The night was sound and it was light. Telescreens flickered in their harsh-hued colors. Ribbons of white tubing ran overhead, bringing the brightness of high noon to the streets, a brightness unrelieved by shadow or warmth. The hills were a mass of light clusters, like a field of white flowers in full bloom. And, as I moved away from a main thoroughfare, car headlights tore great gaps out of darker streets and, as they approached each other, seemed to fence like ancient warriors in swordplay.

I seemed acutely sensitive to all sensation. My eyes ached from the assault of light, my head reverberated with the Saturday night sounds, my body seemed bruised and battered from the jostling of the crowds spilling along the sidewalks. I moved deliberately away into darker, quieter streets, unconscious of weariness, hardly aware of the dull ache of the gash in my arm or the steady throbbing of my head. I stumbled aimlessly through the network of vast apartment projects and sprawling trailer parks, aware of life and laughter and shared enjoyment all around me, of the tightening kiss and the flushed angry face and the quiet amusement and the tension of waiting. I felt intensely alone.

I lost all sense of time. How many miles I walked I don't know. At one time I found myself in a section of the Culver basin of trailer courts that seemed familiar. I wondered if I had once lived here, if I could be near the site of the trailer in which I had grown up with my mother. I found familiar landmarks and, groping along the trail of memory, came upon unfamiliar streets and stores and shining new trailers. Too much had changed. The past was lost, all but a few traces obliterated by the indifferently destructive feet of progress.

Slowly the crowds withdrew. The clamor of the city stilled. Public telescreens clicked off, were seen as massive square patches of gray against the darker sky. The close-packed streams of cars thinned out. The sidewalks emptied except for the occasional straggler. Lights winked out on the hills encircling the city.

I walked alone, a madman, looking as if for the last time at the ugliness, the beauty, the raw scars of love and hate, the broken window of violence, the scented flower of affection.

As dawn broke, I left the normal world of humanity behind me. I caught an almost empty train to the top of the hill. When I reached my trailer, the sun, still invisible behind the eastern range of hills, had set the sky on fire. I stood on the step for a moment, casting a long, searching look at the sleeping city.

Then I went in and closed the door.

20

AT FIRST THE pills seemed to have little effect. In spite of the warning on the bottle I took a third pill. I stared fixedly at the label: K7U. I wondered what the letters symbolized. One part of K to seven parts of U? Or was this the formula arrived at on the seventh try? I tried to read the words printed in Latin on the label. My eyes refused to focus.

Drowsily I lay back on the bed. My eyelids were heavy weights, my legs were leaden. I made an attempt to shift my feet, but I lacked the strength. I seemed to sink deep into the soft folds of the bed. At last I slept.

The day was broken into bright fragments of consciousness projecting out of a woolly fuzz in which I was often neither fully awake nor asleep. The barrier between consciousness and the oblivion of unconsciousness seemed to have disintegrated. At one point—I thought it was in the morning, but the time of day was not important, time itself had ceased to exist—the phone rang incessantly and I wanted desperately to answer it, but I was chained to the bed. And there was a moment when the girl next door was beating upon the window, her mouth twisted in grief. She saw me watching her and she fled. I called after her but there was no sound. At some point in the late afternoon I stood at the window. The sun was a blazing ball in the hard steel plate of sky. It seemed to have not only light and heat but sound, clashing and grinding until my head seemed sure to shatter from the vibrations.

Always in those sharp, isolated moments of crystal clarity, I saw everything with extraordinary vividness. Colors held an intensity I had never seen before—the shimmering green of a patch of grass, the brown of a tree trunk projecting from the yellow hills, the hot red of a plastic chair, the glittering white of a trailer, the shiny yellow-and-black of a police helicopter stuck against the intense blue of the sky. I saw in the most commonplace plant an unimaginable beauty, an exquisite natural architecture of life.

My perspective was faulty. Distances deceived me. Walls that should have met seemed to be in different planes. Space was an illusion. I reached for a glass on a table and missed it completely. Once I tried to sit on a chair and tumbled to the floor. Crawling, I seemed to inch forward over an interminable distance, taking hours to cover the few feet from one side of my living room to another, and this was not at all surprising or disturbing to me. At one time I was sitting on the floor of the kitchen looking up in wonder at the immense cliff of the sink high above me. And again I was walking down the narrow hall between my bedroom and the front of the trailer. The floor wobbled and waved and the hall stretched on endlessly, a bewildering corridor of doors that I kept reaching for and missing, until at last I burst out of the corridor into the bedroom, and then I was falling toward the bed, falling, floating through the cold black infinity of space.

While the hot mid-day sun beat down upon the trailer, I stood indifferently watching the still, white face of my mother, what had been my mother, lying rigid in the meaningless calm of death. I felt a total numbness, an absence of feeling, as if my whole body and brain had been shot with novocain.

But later, much, much later, I stared out at a gray city under a gray sky, relieved only by the streaks of orange and red and purple left by the sun at the horizon, and tears rolled down my face. I cried without knowing why I grieved.

I slept and dreamed of waves washing over me, of voices pounding with the fury of waves, lifting and tossing me at will, thundering and growling. And in the chaos of semi-consciousness, I tasted the delicious sweetness of red lips, felt the incredible softness of breasts crushed against my chest, touched with my fingers the silken mass of red hair—and found it inexplicably turned to gold, to the yellow of a field of grain under a hot August sun.

And in the evening, when darkness crouched like a living thing in the corners of the small bedroom, I woke suddenly to a moment of ordinary reality in which I saw the room

123

exactly as it had always been, saw the open bottle of pills on the built-in chest within arm's reach, smelled the odor of my sweat-drenched body. Bewilderment flooded through me. I had the fleeting thought that this was wrong, that the pills had failed, that the snake pit into which I had plunged had been only an illusion. I groped toward understanding, but sleep descended upon me like a thick black fog. I tried to escape the darkness, grasping at the flickering light of reason, but it fled into the distance like the vanishing light in the center of a television screen turned off, the dot of light swiftly receding into a pinprick of brightness, winking, winking out. . . .

The floor creaked. I woke trembling with an immediate and frightening impression that someone was in the trailer. I was not sure what had awakened me and for a moment I had no memory of the long, lost day. Then the floor creaked again.

And still I didn't understand. In a tumbling confusion of pictures I remembered the pills and the distortions they had produced. As quickly as this memory jelled, I knew that the pills had not worked. They had failed to induce the symptomatic exaggeration of my illness. My reaction had been violent, but it was no more than a normal mind's response to a heavy dosage. Moreover, the effects had worn off too fast.

All this I saw, but its significance escaped me. I was still thinking fuzzily. My head ached with an almost unbearable pressure and my limbs still felt heavy. The third warning creak brought me fully awake, and I knew that someone was creeping along the narrow hall toward me. I could see nothing in the darkness and there was no sound of breathing or of stealthy feet. But the complaining floor was a voice too familiar to be missed. It could mean only one thing.

I waited tensely, straining every sense. Nothing moved. I began to make out shadowy shapes as my eyes adjusted to the dark. Doubts attacked me. Could this be it after all—

the mind's final breaking point? The self-created monster in the darkness?

At last full understanding came. No. I was not insane. The pills had merely proven my sanity. They had done their job after all. The danger now was real. Everything that I had been ready to dismiss as the delusions and hallucinations of a sick mind—all of it was real. And now—

He attacked.

In the instant I knew that I was rational and whole, I was able to move, rolling to the side. A giant figure crashed onto the bed where I had lain. I could hear his hoarse, quick breathing, no longer held in silence. I spun away from him. A huge hand caught at my arm, but I broke free. Still rolling, I tumbled onto the floor. As he pulled himself off the bed, I staggered to my feet. The room reeled around me. The effects of the drug had not fully worn off. I tried to take a step toward the hall and it was like walking through deep water, my steps slow and sluggish. I could see the man towering above me as he leaped off the bed. A great hand grabbed at my suit as I fell away, and the fabric tore. I stumbled, off balance, unable to control the loose flopping of my arms and legs. A fist slashed at me and glanced off my cheek. Even the slashing blow was so powerful that it smashed me backwards, half-stunned, to crash against the wall beside the bed. I went down heavily. My cheekbone felt as if it had been pulverized.

Panic came. The relief which had first soared in me at the knowledge that I was a sane man was lost now in the bitter realization that I had discovered the truth too late. There was no way I could survive this giant's attack. But who was he?

A huge hand plucked me from the floor and flung me down on the bed. He was bending over me then, his hands clutching at my throat. His breath whistled through his open mouth. He shifted, bringing up his thickly-muscled leg to pin me under him. With the desperation of fear and the blind urge to survival, I twisted wildly. One free hand raked at his eyes. He gave a bellow of rage and pain and pulled away, pawing at his face. I wrenched away from the loosening grasp of the hand which still gripped my throat.

I broke past him. It was an immense effort to drag my heavy thighs forward, straining for speed. In the fleeting seconds it took me to stumble to the doorway, I seemed to live an eternity of effort and jumbled thoughts. This was the alien—it must be! No subtleties now, no clever tricks of the mind—just brute force. And I had a vivid picture of Lois Worthington as she must have looked with her neck snapped like a brittle twig. I knew that I would not get away, that this was the end of all my running.

My hand, catching the door frame, brushed against a switch and the room suddenly blazed with light. Over my shoulder I saw him charging after me—saw the shock of black hair, the powerful shoulders and arms, the thick features twisted now in fury. Mike Boyle!

For an instant the light blinded him. And in that moment, out of the confusion and shock of recognition, I had time to feel a surge of disbelief. He couldn't be the one! I knew this slow, arrogant mind. And if he could control me as the alien had, why hadn't he stopped me now from trying to get away?

And then he was lumbering toward me. As I tried to spin away from him along the hall, his big hands pulled me back. I felt his arms slide around my chest and tighten. Twisting, I stared directly into his eyes. They were glazed, unseeing, frighteningly dumb. A crushing pressure squeezed my ribs together. I struggled weakly, kicking at his legs, trying to reach his eyes with my hand. Pain lanced through my chest, increasing swiftly in intensity as the terrible pressure drove the air from my lungs and my chest seemed to cave in.

And through the streaks of pain slipped a stab of perception. He was controlled! This was not the alien. This was a weaker mind, helpless to resist the command which drove him to kill just as I was helpless in his terrible embrace. Here was a weapon I had not counted on, an ultimate weapon beyond resistance—

The pain grew savage. I seemed to hear a cracking of

bones yielding and I thought I could not bear the pain. A stifled, breathless cry broke through my locked jaws. Consciousness began to slip away from me and the trailer seemed to tip slowly like a ship listing.

"There is no pain, no sickness, no evil beyond the power of the mind to control."

The rich, vibrant voice of Swami Fallaninda echoed in the recesses of my mind. *No pain,* I thought dimly. *Concentrate and there will be no pain. Draw the mind in upon itself, obliterate the knowledge of the body's anguish. Concentrate intensively, know the power of your own mind, and there is nothing you cannot do—*

"Stop!"

I flung the mind's command at Boyle with all the force of my wavering consciousness. I felt his powerful body go rigid against me. I had reached him! The impulsive desperate try had broken through the barrier of his mind. He could be controlled! If the alien could do it, why not I?

"Release me!"

His throat worked and he gave a strangled cry. I could see his red face contorting with strain. His crushing arms slackened their hold. I tried to draw myself into a ball, to snuff out all pain, all sensation, everything except the awareness of being, of mind, of mental force. I existed only as awareness.

"Now!" My mind hammered the unspoken command at him. "Release me!"

I felt his arms slip loose like a broken spring uncoiling. Twisting free, I backed away from him down the hall. He stood transfixed, his great bulk filling the narrow space, and I saw in his eyes the dumb pain of an animal goaded into a corner, trapped in an intolerable dilemma of conflict. It was only then that I caught some remote glimmering of the torment my counter-command had produced in his captive mind.

I thought again of the swami's ringing words: "Know your own strength, believe in it, fear not!" The little man no longer seemed ridiculous.

The squeal of a police helicopter's siren shrilled close by—so loud that it seemed to come from almost directly overhead. Its shriek seemed to snap something in Mike Boyle's mind. I felt a shiver of horror, as if I had seen a mind broken even as a neck might snap or a rib crack under pressure.

He plunged toward me. Stumbling out of the corridor, I lost my balance and fell backwards. Boyle brushed past me as if I had not been there. He charged across to the door, clawed at its knob, hurled himself through the opening. His shoulder struck the door frame and he went out staggering.

As I reached the doorway, he was lurching into the street. A spotlight slashed toward him out of the darkness. He darted away from it, but the beam pinned his running figure against the outline of a trailer across the way.

"Halt!" a voice barked.

I caught the dim shape of a black police helicopter, its yellow stripe gleaming dully, and I had time to wonder how the police had got there, and I was aware out of the corner of my eye of light glowing in the next-door trailer. Then Mike Boyle was sprinting down the street, ignoring the warning shout, dodging like a halfback through an open field, moving his bulk with startling agility and speed.

Low and vicious, a policeman's silenced special spat out of the darkness. Boyle's legs went out from under him as if he had been hit by a low, hard tackle. The smack as he hit the pavement was brutally audible. Echoing it, so close that it brought me spinning around, was a low cry.

I stared into the frightened eyes of the blonde girl next door. She stood barely two paces away. I had a sudden intuition as if she had spoken to me aloud.

"You called the police," I said.

She nodded. "I—I was afraid you were being hurt."

"But how did you know? How could you know what was happening?"

Her gaze wavered and she seemed to hesitate. The words tumbled out in a rush. "I heard noises—I got up to see what was going on and—and I saw someone trying to break into your trailer, so I—I called the police. That's all."

For a second I frowned at her, trying to read her eyes. She was not frightened at all, I thought with surprise. Elusive. Evasive. Hiding something.

I heard a bellow of rage behind me and turned to see Mike Boyle struggling to get to his feet while two policemen pinned him to the pavement. I sprinted toward them. When I reached the group, Boyle's struggles were growing weaker. There was blood on the paving and I saw it seeping down his leg. He was mouthing unintelligible sounds and his eyes had that strange, glazed, unseeing stare. I looked at the two policemen holding him and recognized the pair who had questioned me earlier. Sgt. Bullock's cold, hard face had regained its meanness. I wondered what had become of the friendly puppy I had met the day before.

"What's this all about?" he snapped. "Who is he?"

"His name is Boyle," I said. "He's a student at the university—a football star. He's—he's out of his mind."

"*Mike* Boyle?" The sergeant's tone was incredulous.

"Yes. And Sergeant—" I weighed the words carefully, "I think he killed Lois Worthington."

Slowly the sergeant stood up. His eyes were mean slits in the blunt face. "You better know what you're saying," he said. "You goddam well better know."

For an instant I faltered, less sure of myself. I had no real evidence that Boyle had murdered the waitress, nothing but the faith I now had in my own convictions. But I knew without question that he had been ordered to kill her just as he had been directed to eliminate me. Yet I couldn't tell the police how I knew. If I tried to tell them the whole story, I would merely convince them that I was crazy.

The sergeant strode away. He reached the helicopter and pulled out a hand mike. I looked down at Boyle. He lay still, no longer struggling. Some of the bestial panic seemed to have drained out of his face. When I glanced up the sergeant was charging back toward me.

"Well?" he barked as he reached me. "What makes you say he killed the girl?"

"It was—something he said—when he was trying to kill me."

"Why would he try to kill you?"

I made my decision. "I think he blamed me—he was convinced that I had had something to do with Lois."

"Yeah?" Sgt. Bullock's hard, narrow gaze held mine. "Funny you should say that. I thought you were mixed up in this right from the beginning—and I'm beginning to think so again. It's nice and convenient for you to come up with another killer. The guy we were holding—Harry Grayson—cleared himself. The truth tests proved it right down the line. He's not guilty. He didn't kill her."

I stared again at Boyle. Handcuffed now, he was watching me. There was fright in his small eyes and it seemed to me that there was something stirring now in their depths that had been filmed over before, a glimmer of reason.

"Boyle did it," I said. "But he wasn't responsible for what he did. You can see that."

"Yeah? Maybe." The sergeant stared suspiciously at me. "What happened to your head?"

"I was in an accident—in a car."

"Yeah? You seem to be in a hell of a lot of accidents. I think maybe you better come downtown with us. You got quite a lot of explaining to do. You keep popping up in this too often, Cameron. I don't like coincidences."

"I killed her!" Boyle blurted out.

We all stared at him—Bullock, his lean partner, myself. The big youth rolled over on his side. Tears spilled down his cheeks and he began to beat his head against the pavement with a terrifying deliberateness.

"I killed her, I killed her," he moaned. "I killed her!"

The corporal bent down swiftly and jerked Boyle's head up. Sgt. Bullock moved in quickly. Between them they held the big man immobile.

"Okay," the sergeant said after a moment, glancing at me over his shoulder. "So he did it. So maybe that lets you

130

out. We won't need you tonight—but stay where I can find you. I've still got some questions to ask you."

"What about him? What are you going to do with him?"

"There's an ambulance on the way." He looked past me, his gaze sweeping in a circle. "If you want to help you can tell these people to go back to bed. Then you might as well do the same."

I discovered that a large number of people had come out of their trailers and were standing in clusters talking and staring curiously at the tableau in the street. For some reason I was surprised. The whole incident had happened so quickly and with so little noise that I hadn't thought of anyone being aroused.

I moved toward the nearest group. "It's all over," I said quietly. "Might as well go back to bed."

"What happened?"

"A man went—" I caught myself. "Just a drunk. A guy who had more than he could take."

The groups of people gave way slowly, reluctantly. I stared back once more at Mike Boyle. I felt only pity now. At the same time I was aware of how timely and how lucky for me had been his guilt-ridden outcry of confession. Without it, I would have been in more trouble than I liked to think about, with Bullock eager to jump all over me, firing questions which I couldn't answer.

Boyle would be cured. His illness was not a deep-seated mental aberration but a temporary cracking under pressure. They would treat him and, when he was rational, they would get a full confession out of him about the murder of Lois. But they would never make sense out of his story of being controlled by an inhuman mind. He would get off on the plea of insanity. They would cure him and when they were sure that he was well, he would be freed.

I wondered if he would remember or understand later what had been done to him. Or who had done it.

Looking up, I saw the girl next door standing where I had left her. I walked slowly toward her. In her eyes and mouth I read anxiety.

"He tried to kill you," she whispered.

I nodded. I felt an inexpressible tenderness. Gratitude, I thought. How much I owed to her!

"Thanks for calling the police," I said. "And for—for being worried."

She blushed. Even in the darkness I could see the bright color in her cheeks. She started to turn away and the movement of her hips brought back, sharply and vividly, the image I had seen through her window so long ago.

"Wait!"

She stopped, her face averted, and I caught once again the sense of a bird trembling on the brink of flight.

"I don't even know your name," I said gently.

Her voice was low. "Erika," she said. "Erika Lindstrom."

I smiled. The name so perfectly suited her tall, blonde beauty. I felt a renewal of that strange, deep rush of tender feeling.

"Thanks again, Erika."

"Goodnight, Mr. Cameron," she said quickly.

This time I didn't try to stop her. Watching her retreat into the security of her trailer, I wondered why she was so anxious to help me. The knowledge of her anxiety gave me an unfamiliar pulsation of pleasure. In that moment I felt that I had regained more than my faith in my own reason. I had recaptured something lost long ago. Closeness. Warmth. The touch of humanity.

21

SLEEP HAD COME to me suddenly—deep, exhausted sleep. The annoying sound nagged at the edges of my subconscious for a long time. I became remotely aware of it, a buzzing far off, droning on interminably. Vainly I tried to escape it, to bury myself in the soft, black, velvet cushion of sleep, but the sound penetrated—a thin, distant, persistent plea.

And I woke. It was still night. The same night? Or could

I have slept the clock around? I peered at the luminous time and date dials in the wall. It was almost three in the morning. I had slept for less than five hours. Five hours before, I had escaped death. Time enough for a new plan to be laid.

The phone rang again. With a groan of exasperation, I dragged myself out of the bed and groped my way into the living room. Through bleary, heavy-lidded eyes I tried to make out the reception button, hit it on the third jab.

"Hello? Paul? Is that you?"

The image on the telephone screen was still dim. It brightened as I stared in disbelief.

"Laurie! What in God's name are you doing calling me at this hour?"

"Oh, Paul! Thank God!"

She sagged visibly. Even on the black-and-white screen her face showed pale and drawn, with a sharpness I had never seen in it before.

"What is it. What's happened?"

"I've been trying to get you for hours. You've got to help me. You've got to come out here!"

I felt the first premonition of danger, a warning signal in the back of my mind echoing the phone's buzz of a moment earlier. Peering narrowly at the screen I tried to shake off the fuzziness of drugged sleep.

"Tell me what's wrong," I said sharply.

"I—I can't. Please, Paul!" She began to cry silently, bending over, hugging her stomach as if she were in pain. "Please!"

I strained to see into the room behind her but her image filled most of the screen. I stared closely at her. She was in her nightgown. It had fallen off one bare shoulder and was tied loosely around her waist. Her long red hair spilled free around her shoulders. She looked as if she had been in bed. Something had aroused her—something frightening. There was no mistaking the haggard aspect of fear. She seemed to be holding herself together with an anguished effort of control.

"Is there anyone with you?" I asked quietly.

She shook her head—too quickly, I thought. Something moved in my abdomen. Fear coiling.

"Paul, help me!" she moaned. "You've got to help me. There's nobody else who can."

"You're at the beach house?" I asked, stalling, angry at the cowardice that made me delay.

"Yes, yes! Alone! I'm all alone. You'll come? You'll come right away?" Her voice grew shrill with eager hope. "I'll do anything, darling, anything you ever want me to do. I love you! You know that, don't you? You believe that? I didn't mean the things I said last night. Paul, I'll do anything!"

You don't have to keep saying it, I thought. You don't have to bribe me. I wondered with dull anger how long it had taken to affect the careless arrangement of her nightgown.

And then I repented of the impulse which had momentarily made me despise her. How could such a beautiful, spoiled child be asked to have more strength and courage than I myself had shown? I couldn't deny her the hope that cried out in her words, the terrified plea that was expressed in every straining curve of her body. I couldn't refuse to help her. For this was not an alien. This was another helpless human being whose life had touched mine, and who was now, because of that briefly intimate contact, in a state of almost mindless panic.

Mindless. I remembered Mike Boyle and how viciously he had been used.

"Yes," I said flatly. "I'll help you. I'll come."

She began to babble in an hysteria of relief, the words tumbling meaninglessly over each other. Love. Darling. Help me. Anything you want. Alone. Come. Please. Anything, anything, anything. I didn't bother to listen. When she had run down I stared at the young, lovely, tear-stained face and felt an inexpressible pity.

"You don't have to worry," I said. "I'll be there."

I did not want to go. When I thought about what I would

find on that isolated beach, I cringed inside. It was no good pretending the fear did not exist, but I pushed it into a corner and tried not to look at it.

And yet I had to consider some facts. How vulnerable were the aliens? What weapons would touch them? If the bodies in which they lived were destroyed, would the aliens perish? Or did they so infuse and inform their hosts that their apparently human forms became immune to the violence which would destroy an ordinary human body? From the conversation overheard in the Dugout I had acquired the vague idea that somehow the furious energy of the aliens sapped the very flesh of the hosts they inhabited. One of them had urged the other to maintain a tight, constant control over the body to keep it from—what had he said?— to keep it from disintegrating. To hold it together. What did that mean? Could a mind hold matter in a fixed state, retaining an exterior form, when there was no longer any intrinsic unity of the body? Mind over matter, mind ruling matter. The possibility was not so fantastic. It was even a subject of scientific inquiry on earth.

But what weapons might affect a body so controlled? Would a bullet smashing into that occupied brain destroy the alien's hold? I had no way of knowing. In any event I didn't have a gun. It would have to be some other weapon.

I made a hasty but thorough search of my trailer. I took a small knife with a retractable blade from a drawer in the kitchen. As I pulled open other drawers and rummaged through them, I kept wishing that I had had the sense to arm myself with some kind of pistol. My choice of weapons was pitifully limited. In the bottom drawer of a small cabinet built into the corridor, among a jumbled collection of tools and gadgets, I found a small pocket flame-thrower, one of those all-purpose gas-fired lighters that is adjustable for the small flame needed to light a cigarette or the steady blaze that will ignite charcoal for a fire or even a miniature jet of heat suitable to cut thin pieces of metal. I started to discard the gadget but some obscure tug of memory stopped me. Heat. Heat brought more than searing pain. It consumed. All living organisms were vulnerable to it. On those planets where the temperature was too high, scientists agreed, life could not exist.

I stuck the little flame-thrower in my pocket. At least some of the time I had spent in the library had not been wasted, I thought, though the gadget seemed ridiculously small and ineffectual as a potential weapon against super-human beings.

The rest of my search was fruitless. I didn't let myself dwell on the futility of the weapons I had. If I did that I wouldn't go out. I would cower in a corner of the trailer with my panic and wait for them to come after me. It was better to face them in the open and with what protection the darkness of night might afford.

I slipped on a coverall, shoes and a light windproof jacket. I turned out all the lights and stood by the door in the living room. It crossed my mind that I might never be returning to these small rooms. The thought left me strangely unmoved. I opened the door quietly and stepped out into the cold and the darkness.

Walking along the road toward the elevated station, I glanced back once. A light shone yellow and misty, its rays radiating like a stain in the dark mist. I stopped, thinking that I had failed to turn off all the lights. Checking back in my mind I remembered the total darkness the moment before I stepped out of the trailer. This light, then, had just gone on. It wasn't from one of my rooms.

The girl next door was awake, once again aware of everything I was doing. It was uncanny. I was convinced that I hadn't made enough noise to awaken her. Unless she had been lying wide-eyed and sleepless, listening. But why? With a shrug of impatience, I turned away from the puzzle and hurried along the deserted road toward the station.

I stepped up to the landing platform cautiously. One slim tube of light ran overhead, dimmed now by the curling mist. There was no one else on the platform. I checked the night schedule listed on the board and saw that a local beach train was due in seven minutes. I was in luck. There wouldn't be another beach local for forty minutes after this one. I pressed the night pickup light and saw its red warning glow a quarter-mile away down the monorail.

A feeling of tension increased as the minutes ticked by. Little could happen to me here on this platform except for that one split-second when the train would slide in front of me, and it was unlikely that there was any danger. They wouldn't go to all the trouble of pretending to lure me to the beach if they wanted to kill me in my own back yard. Nevertheless I kept far back from the edge of the platform, and when I first heard the rush of the approaching train, the muscles tightened involuntarily in my chest and arms.

Then the serpentine column of the train slid swiftly into the station, braking fast, and I saw the warm glow of the lighted interior, the familiar sight of passengers dozing or staring out the windows. I stepped into the train and, seconds later, while I walked toward a seat at the rear of the car, the train was once more speeding away over the ridge of the hills, the momentum of its plunge hardly detectible inside the car.

There were very few travelers at this time of night. It was too early for the night shifts to be getting out, too late for revelers to be coming home. There were a half-dozen people in my car but none of them paid any attention to me after the first curious glance. I felt the tension easing in my body.

Most of the time, the thick early morning mist hid the sleeping city that lay at the foot of the hills. Occasionally I caught glimpses of light patterns far below through open patches in the fog. But generally there were no landmarks visible, not even the familiar yawning canyons or the sculptured back of the hills, and I kept getting a peculiar feeling of isolation, of rushing through a void. I thought of the men who had cruised through the infinite emptiness of space between Earth and Mars, little dreaming on their return that they brought two stowaways. How had the aliens concealed themselves? Dr. Temple's logical arguments meant little now. Somewhere there was a flaw, a crack in the wall of checks and precautions through which the aliens had slipped. I knew that I had been driven by a compulsion to face the inevitable decisive clash with the enemy. I had had to come in answer to Laurie's plea, knowing that I was probably walking into a trap. Choice really hadn't played a part in my decision. This was the inescapable moment toward which I had been compelled by everything that had happened to me—not just in the recent crowded days but in the months I had listened to the whispered voices in my mind and wondered, in the nights when I had awakened shivering from the dream.

Yes. The dream. This too I had to face. The smashing waves, the dominating voice. For an instant, remembering, I felt again the weight of hopelessness. Just as quickly I rejected it. The dream need not have been clairvoyant. It could have been a subconscious projection of my fear of the voices I had heard—and my tormenting doubt that the voices existed. No. I couldn't think about the dream. And this time the aliens would not be confronting a dumbly acquiescent, frightened animal. They were not invincible. This time the clash might be a little more equal. Unless—

A quick contraction of muscles shattered my illusion that I had conquered the fear. Unless both of the aliens would be there for the kill. I forced myself to examine the possibility rationally. The older one, the leader, did not want them to be together unless it was absolutely necessary. And why should they believe that handling me would require two superior minds? One would be enough. No, the young one would be alone, the junior partner, who wouldn't admit being unable to eliminate me without difficulty.

The reflection stirred me to a fresh sensation, a stubborn, smoldering anger.

22

THERE WAS A LOCAL stop less than a half-mile south of the Beachcomber Trailer Lodge. I made no move. The train slid smoothly along its single overhead rail once more. Seconds later, when I guessed that we had traveled less than a mile, I rose, walked quickly to the end of the car and jabbed the emergency stop signal. While the few sleepy passengers in the car were staring at me, startled, the train came to one of its gently quivering sudden stops. I stepped on the floor panel just inside the narrow emergency exit. A door slid open. Damp, salt-smelling ocean mist swirled in through the door. Dropping quickly to the floor, I eased myself over the edge. For several seconds I hung by my arms in mid-air outside the car, my hands gripping the door sill. In the thick mist I couldn't see the ground below. From inside the car someone shouted. The emergency door started to close and I dropped.

Falling through space I endured a slowly turning moment of panic. I had misjudged the distance! Then I hit the ground with a jarring force that seemed to unhinge my jaws. I tumbled and rolled, slamming finally to a stop against a solid wall of earth. Breathless and dazed, I lay peering up at the train. The emergency door opened again and a uniformed man stood framed in the oblong panel of yellow light some fifteen feet overhead. He muttered angrily. Although he appeared to be looking directly at me, I was sure that he couldn't see me. After a moment he drew back inside. The door closed. After a brief interval the train eased into motion, humming softly as it gathered speed. The last car vanished abruptly and I was alone in the thick black silence. I could feel a throbbing in my left arm. Something wet trickled into the crook of my elbow and I realized that the still-fresh cut had reopened.

Painfully I pushed myself erect. Now I could hear the noisy clamor of the surf nearby. The mist curled and eddied around me, dense patches giving way to open gaps through which I caught the wet reflection of pavement. I tried to orient myself. The monorail was on the inland side of the beach highway. I would probably have to follow the road back to Laurie's trailer community. I had intended to come up to it along the beach, but in this fog there was little chance that I would find or recognize her trailer group.

I set off along the road. There was no traffic at all. When I had been walking for ten minutes I began to realize that I had underestimated the train's speed. I had overshot the Beachcomber Lodge by more than I had thought. Still I didn't regret the decision not to get out at the station. There, I would have been too vulnerable, making a public announcement of my arrival. At least now I had the faint possibility of surprise.

From the edge of the road I could barely make out the lighted signs which spelled out the names of the different trailer parks, their letters hardly distinguishable blurs in the mist. This wasn't like the dream, I thought, unable to disguise a quick surge of relief. Everything had been clear in the dream. I walked on slowly, cautiously, feeling the damp cold steal through the fabric of my coverall and jacket. And at last, winking at me from a flat hollow of the beach, I saw the sign: BEACHCOMBER TRAILER LODGE.

I stopped. Trying to open my mind to every impulse, I stood motionless, thinking of nothing, waiting and listening. There was only the steady, rhythmic roll and crash of the ocean beating against the edge of the land. There was no foreign whisper of sound, no strange vibration of thought. Nothing out of the ordinary. Yet I felt danger around me like a physical presence. Some unfathomed ear of the mind heard and telegraphed its message to the taut nerves of my body. I began to tremble. It's the cold, I thought angrily, gritting my teeth to stop their chattering. It's this damned cold wet fog.

Moving now in a crouch, I turned and retraced my steps to a point a hundred yards north of the Beachcomber's sign. There I scrambled down the incline from the road to the lower level where trailers huddled close like motionless animals hiding in the protective mist. I made my way carefully among them until I reached the empty strip of beach fringing the ocean. Here the roar of the waves was almost deafening, magnified in the darkness and the silence of the night. Dimly, I could make out the white foam boiling up the wet slope toward me. I had to fight down the cringing panic, holding my mind closed like a steel trap against the invasion of memory, against the terror of the dream whose vivid details crowded forward, demanding to be seen and heard and felt.

My body rigid with the tension of enforced discipline, I crept along the beach, counting my steps, measuring the distance until I knew I had covered the hundred yards and must be opposite the sign which faced the highway, invisible now in the dark gray soup of mist lying over the beach. I stopped, trying to place exactly in my mind the location of Laurie's trailer. It was in the front row of trailers facing the beach, half-concealed behind the swelling curve of a dune. I remembered being able to see the surface of the water from the raised interior of the trailer but being cut off from it by the dune when I was standing outside. And it seemed to me that, entering the trailer park from the highway, I had followed a curving walk toward the left.

I saw the patch of light through a gap in the mist not more than thirty yards away. It was blotted out almost instantly. I edged forward and away from the shoreline, moving onto slightly higher ground. The mist tore again and I saw the window clearly, its glow touching the swirling fog outside with a pale phosphorescence. The bright window seemed a warm invitation, not dangerous at all.

For perhaps a full minute I crouched motionless on the cold sand while the mist curled around me. Every sense strained to detect the unseen menace lurking behind the veil of darkness. Nothing. Not a sound, not a quiver of sensation, not a single vibrating wave of thought.

I began to inch forward. The light grew closer, visible now as a blurred rectangle even through the dense portions of the fog. With each step that brought me nearer to the beckoning rectangle of light, I could feel my heart beat faster, louder.

It stopped in that instant when I rose to bring my eyes over the edge of the window. It tripped and caught again like a sluggish motor. I could feel its labored thudding in my temples.

Laurie sat huddled in a corner of the room. Her green eyes were wide open, staring fixedly at the door. In her hand was a small pistol, squat and ugly, its muzzle pointing across the room. No one else was in sight. I frowned suspiciously. Then I realized that the fear radiating from the whole attitude of her body was directed and focused on something outside the room, beyond the door. And I knew that the gun was for me.

Cautiously I circled the trailer. I saw no shadow stirring. I paused outside the door, listening. I stood clear of it and reached out to turn the knob. It wasn't locked. The door swung open easily under the pressure of my hand. I jumped back as the pistol spoke, its bark low and sharp. The bullet struck metal somewhere behind me and ricocheted, whining off into the darkness. I was already moving forward up the steps and into the trailer.

"Drop it, Laurie!"

I looked into the muzzle of the pistol. It wavered unsteadily. Laurie didn't move. The cords of her throat were working visibly and I sensed the horror of a scream frozen inside of her by muscles that refused to function.

"Drop it!"

The gun fell from nerveless fingers and clattered to the floor. I crossed the room quickly and reached for Laurie's shoulders.

"Laurie! Laurie—"

The scream found a slim opening, sliced through not as a full-throated cry but as a thin high wail of terror. She shrank away from me. Her dressing gown fell open at the throat as she drew back. Half-naked, her eyes fixed and blank with fright, she cowered in the corner. I could see the shudders pass along her body. I caught her by the arms and pulled her erect, holding her tightly.

"I'm here, Laurie," I said hoarsely. "Paul. I came. There's nothing to be afraid of any more. I'm here."

I spoke with a confidence I did not feel, but something

in the urgency of my voice reached her. Suddenly she collapsed against me. A sob tore from her throat and then she was crying, openly and without control, tears bathing her cheeks while the deep sobs wrenched her body. I held her, stroking her shoulders and her back gently, murmuring soothing meaningless phrases. And slowly the terror seemed to draw back inside her, subsiding to an occasional quiver, until at last the flow of tears dried up and her eyes were empty.

I drew her over to the couch and sat beside her, holding her hands. Her fingers gripped mine with involuntary tension like the grasping fingers of a baby.

"Can you tell me what happened? Laurie, can you hear me? Do you know what I'm saying?"

A spasm shook her. I spoke quickly, gently.

"You don't have to be afraid any more. You won't be harmed. Do you understand that?"

Her eyes were wide and staring. Her lips were slack, red slashes trembling in the bloodless white of her face. I squeezed her hands.

"Laurie!" I said sharply. "How long ago was it? When did it happen?"

Her lips moved soundlessly. She began to shake again, to vibrate like an animal too terrified to run.

"Who did it, Laurie? Who made you call me? Who wanted you to kill me?"

I knew it was hopeless to question her even as my hands gripped her shoulders and shook her. She couldn't answer. In a deep state of shock, exuding fear, she could hardly be aware of what I asked. But I didn't need her reply. I already knew.

And I felt the anger growing in me, active and violent, a deep revulsion and a raging hatred for the alien things to whom human beings were simply inferior organisms to be possessed and used, discarded or destroyed. Looking down at Laurie, at this young and slim and beautiful woman, at the vivid red hair spilling over white quivering shoulders, I knew that what I felt for her was not love but something

143

equally important, sympathy and compassion and a strong affection that could easily, under other circumstances, erupt into desire and need. I felt linked with her in a common humanity and a common anger.

And I hated what I had to do to her.

I picked up the small pistol which had fallen from her fingers. For a moment I was tempted to discard the plan which had formed itself in my mind. Perhaps it wouldn't be necessary. Perhaps I could squeeze the trigger myself before my finger froze in the paralysis of obedience.

No. There was only one slim chance. It might fail but I had to risk it. I had to try to turn the alien's own weapon against it.

"Laurie," I said gently. "Listen to me."

I spoke to her then without words.

23

THE CHALLENGE CAME. It was quite close, coming from out there in the mist and the darkness, strong and cold and relentless. It pulled me across the room. I jerked open the door. As I stepped out into the night I heard Laurie give a whimpering cry. Ahead of me the pounding surf beckoned. I felt the unwanted constriction of fear but I felt something more— human pride and defiance.

It was chill and damp and dark as a mine on the beach. The heavy mist was moist against my face. I stood facing the pulsations of the alien mind and slowly, like the curtain rising on a play, the mist began to lift. With a fog's capriciousness, it rose above my head and stopped to hang suspended over the beach, revealing now the white curve of sand, the black swell of waves, the dim gray shapes of trailers, but still blotting out the hills rising beyond.

And I saw her—a slim, small figure some fifty paces away, standing very straight, a figure of fragile innocence. I thought with pity of the young girl she once had been, the girl now soul-destroyed, the human named Helen Darrow.

I felt no surprise. How easily I had been duped! I wondered if her parents knew what she was or if they too were puppets dancing on a string, playing a perfect pantomime of human life. And then I severed all these cords of thought, cutting off the smell and taste and touch of the sea air, opening my mind to the vibrations beating against it, seeing not with my eyes but with the sightless vision of the mind.

I saw a coldness which wore the mask of hate but had not hatred's feeling. My spirit shriveled at the sight of the ugliness, the vicious indifference of the alien mind. An instinctive repugnance made me recoil as if, feeling blindly in the grass, I had touched the cold white belly of a snake. At that moment the alien struck.

"Drown!" The voice spoke.

"No!" I shouted aloud. "Not this time!"

The alien lashed out again, its overpowering vibrations forming words that were in my mind but not of it. "Drown! Drown yourself!"

My feet dug into the sand. I braced myself against the thundering echo in my ear.

"Walk! Now! Into the water!"

The strange motionless struggle continued, two minds locked in conflict in that first struggle for mastery, like two wrestlers testing strength, standing with feet spread wide, thick legs firm, hand linked behind each other's neck, muscles bulging as the heads and shoulders bend under the pressure, until the greater strength begins to tell and in the weaker man a foot shifts suddenly, the corded forearms begin to tremble, he feels himself slipping, weakening, falling as the force comes down hard and strong and overpowering.

Tears blinded me. The alien voice obliterated thought, blotting out the frustration and the anger and the pride. And one foot moved. A feeble protest formed in familiar words as I spoke to myself, to the robot body that had always been mine to command. Now the body heard another voice, was deaf to the child's protesting cry.

"Walk! Walk! Walk!"

145

And I lived the dream of long ago, the nightmare which had brought me here to the final crisis, the vision I had known would come true. I felt the remembered numbing cold around my ankles, rising swiftly in a cascade of foam. My feet dragging in the heavy surf, each step a battle lost, each movement a breach smashed in the crumbling wall of my will. I saw on the beach the alien enemy, cold, merciless, all-powerful, and the consciousness that I had lost even before I had begun to fight struck me down. My knees gave way and a toppling breaker tore my feet from under me.

I rose out of the water to fight and lose again. And slowly I was driven out to meet the deep black oblivion of the sea. Rigidly I kept my mind locked against the one remaining hope. I walked, a broken, tottering shell of resistance, without strength.

"Walk! Drown! Drown!"

And the undertow joined its tugging weight to the pressure of the mind that drove me. The water swelled and dipped, rose at last above my head and I went under. I had failed. Now it was over. Defeat and the knowledge of hopelessness pushed me deeper. Now I could cease to fight. Now I could give myself to the freezing numbness that stunned my flesh. Now I could taste the warming draught of memory, relive in the final instant of existence all that I had ever known and felt and dreamed, all that I had loved and lost—

The feeble spark of life still flickered. Mind and body rebelled against obliteration. I struggled weakly, straining upwards, steeling my mind against the final, crushing blow of the alien mind.

Its voice was silent.

I dared not believe the sudden stab of reviving hope. For only a moment I existed in what seemed a mental vacuum, hardly realizing that this was but the normal state of the mind's autonomy. My eyes were open to the cold wet sting of the salt water. I could see the brightness above me near the surface. Lungs straining to burst, I thrust suddenly toward the surface. There was a chance. It might have worked!

I burst like a bubble into the open, gulped life-giving air, my chest heaving convulsively. I went under again as the bosom of the ocean heaved in a giant swelling. I came up sputtering.

"Swim back!"

The alien spoke once more in my mind. My arms and legs began to move automatically. They felt as if they were weighted down. I tried to grasp the meaning of the new command. The voice had not been stilled, but—

"Swim! Swim!"

Confused, still unable to control my limbs, I struck out weakly toward the shore, was caught by the gathering thunderhead of a breaker and carried swiftly forward, only to fall behind as the foaming crest rushed on. Another wave picked me up like a bobbing cork and flung me onward, arms threshing. In the torrent of the smashing waves another tumult raged in my mind, a bewilderment of questions and brightening hope.

"Swim!"

I caught the panic in the alien cry, sensed that the call was weaker. The strength of exultation surged in my arms. With a renewed vigor, I drove on to reach the peak of a swiftly rolling wave and soared in like a surfboard on the rushing crest, was flung ahead to tumble head over heels in the churning uproar of the broken wall of water. And now the water rushed swiftly back away from me, receding down the slope of the shore, and I was kneeling on my hands and knees just a few steps away from the glistening sand of the shoreline. I dragged myself up and staggered forward, stumbled, felt the strength go out of my legs and fell face downward on the sand.

"Get up!" The alien voice spoke feebly. "Come here!"

I raised my head. The being housed in the body of Helen Darrow crouched on the wet sand thirty feet away. Her face was grotesquely white like the painted mask of a clown, her eyes huge black holes in the white mask. She was pressing one hand tightly to her side and against the pale color of her dress I saw a darker stain. My gaze swung up the beach.

147

Laurie Hendricks lay inert, sprawled forward on her face. Beyond her outflung hand something metallic glittered on the sand. The gun! Triumph burst full blown in my mind. It had worked! While the alien fought to drive me into the sea, Laurie, obedient to the impulse I had planted in her mind, had crept unnoticed from her trailer and—

But what had happened to her? What had I done to her? "Come here!"

The thought struck viciously with a desperate strength. I looked again at the alien's twisted face, at the arm held out toward me in dramatic repetition of the call to come. And at the end of the outstretched arm was a crumbling stump. There was no hand!

I fought then with all the power that still remained in me, sensing that I had almost won, driving from my mind the horror that beckoned me, admitting no thought save the single dominant denial of the alien call. And still the overwhelming pull of the strange vibrations dragged me forward—one, two, three painful steps. There I held. I felt the momentary flutter of her terror, saw a strange vision of the frozen state of death, and from the alien's weakness found the power to hold. She was dying! Life was pouring out of the mortally wounded body—and the thing pulsating within wanted me! Wanted my body! *Needed* it!

I held and knew the rising pulsation of its fear. The force which pulled at me grew weaker. At last it hesitated, lashed out weakly, stopped. The alien mind drew in upon itself. The vibrations of its panic hammered at me without the power to move.

I stood motionless and watched the girl die. In the final moment of life she gave a human cry. The body toppled forward and rolled over on its back.

The pulsations of the alien mind went on. I felt them now as pain, wave after wave of wordless vibrations beating in my brain until my eyes filmed over. I blinked against the tears. Through the blur, the body on the sand seemed to lose its distinguishable shape, to shed its human form, to disintegrate in the way that the trunk of a hollow, rotten tree eaten away from within will present a smooth, untarnished shell to the eye until one day a sudden blow smashes the outer crust and the tenuous hold of form is broken and the whole tree topples, collapses, dank smelling, into a soft and shapeless heap of dust and debris.

And I saw the alien. It flowed like saliva from the open mouth, flowed out and began to spread, out of the mouth that was no longer a mouth but a shapeless hole in the face that was caving in upon itself. Rigid with horror, I saw the body dissolve into powder. And among the soft crumbling bones moved a thing of dazzling colors, a network of glistening chains of cells spreading like the fingers of a spider web. Salt spray blew over it and the dust of the decaying body stirred like ashes in the wind. I saw the faintly gleaming, almost transparent membranes that joined the network of cell fingers. Drops of water from the spray clung to the filmy membranes like dew. The thing spread like a stain upon the sand, groping among the powdery remains of Helen Darrow's body, reaching out, stretching astonishingly.

Then it began to shrink, to draw its fingers in, folding in upon itself, its movements jerky now, stiffening. The clamor of the alien voice grew shrill. A probing tentacle touched the gray wet body of a dead fish washed up on the shore. With blinding speed the membraneous web contracted upon the fish, enveloping it in a tissue-thin film that seemed to part and shrink as the alien invaded the foreign body, oozing through the gaping mouth. I saw the white slit of a cut on the belly of the fish and stared incredulous as the gash began to close, knitting together, the wound healing as the alien exerted its terrifying power upon the dormant flesh.

With a soft, wet squish, the dead body of the fish exploded, unable to contain the hideous force. My skin crawled with revulsion. This was a power of which I could not have dreamed, a force which had invaded a human body, sapping its very fibers, devouring it from within while holding its matter together until the last spark of life was snuffed out, the alien's hold broken by the bullet from Laurie's gun smashing into the decayed body. Sickness twisted in my stomach. I swayed dizzily. The strumming vibrations of the alien mind shivered through my head, soundless yet like an unendurable, endless screech.

And still I could not move as the alien flowed again on the wet sand, drawing together as a cluster of frothy bubbles, spreading out once more, the moist membranes hardly visible, the rainbow-hued strings of its web-like body reaching, groping blindly, creeping toward me, closer and closer. And a small sand crab scuttled toward it across the sand between us. Sweating and shaking, I watched the hard-shelled creature crawl toward its unseen enemy. A claw touched the moist tissue and the alien struck with sudden violence, silent and terrible, enveloping, smothering, invading the helpless body.

At last I moved. Looking around wildly I saw a chunk of jagged rock half buried in the sand. I pawed it loose. The crab, possessed now, turned a beady eye toward me as I swung around. The painful pulsing in my mind rose harrowingly. With a choking sob of fury I smashed the rock down upon the crab, raised it and smashed down again and again and again, burying the broken, pulpy body in the sand. A sticky piece of protoplasm flew through the air and stuck to my wrist. I brushed it off and it adhered to my fingers like a living thing. I saw the glitter of a tiny string of beads. It moved.

Acting without thought, I clawed in my pocket with my free hand and grasped the small metal cylinder of the pocket lighter. I jerked it out and pressed the button on the end. A thin blue finger of fire danced from the nozzle. I turned the flame upon my fingers where the sticky bit of substance stirred. In my mind there was a snap and shriek like a violin string breaking. Gritting my teeth against the searing pain of the burning flesh, I shook my fingers. The blackened thing dropped off.

I bent down to direct the flame upon the smashed remains of the crab where the alien still crawled. I held it there until at last I was struck by silence. The pulsations were gone. I stared down at the contracted body of the alien.

At first my mind could register only shocked disbelief. What I saw was so familiar that I could not comprehend its meaning. I thought I must be truly mad. Glittering on the wet sand was a small hard cluster of surfaces arranged into the frozen patterns of ordinary rock crystals. On impulse I turned the blue jet of fire upon the chunk. It blackened slowly. At first there seemed to be an infinitesimal shrinking, then only a dark discoloration. When at last I stood erect, turning off the lighter, I knew this alien mind was silenced forever.

I stared down at the blackened chunk of crystals, trying to sort out all the answers that crowded through the suddenly opened door in my mind. This much I knew for certain—strange rock and crystal formations had been brought back from Mars. I had seen them carefully placed on their shelves behind special glass doors. I remembered how strikingly beautiful they had appeared in their dazzling interplay of light and color.

With a shudder I thought of the scientist's habit of touching strange crystals with the tongue.

When I reached Laurie, she was already stirring. I felt an intense relief. Oblivious of the throbbing burn in my left hand, I knelt beside her and put my arm under her shoulders to raise her to a sitting position. Fainting had saved her life—and mine. If she had been conscious the alien would not have needed *my* body. He would have had no need to call me back from the grave.

"Laurie? Can you hear me?"

Her eyes fluttered open, widened as she recognized me. I felt her stiffen.

"It's all right now. She's dead. Because of you. Because you helped me—"

She wrenched violently away from my supporting arm, cringing back from me. "Don't touch me!"

Her voice was shrill with hysteria.

151

"There's nothing to be afraid of," I said soothingly. "It's all over now."

I put out my hand and she began to whimper. "No! No, don't! You're—you're one of them!"

The accusation stunned me.

"You're one of them!" Her mouth began to quiver. I saw the bloodless lips, the glazed eyes of shock and fear. "Please," she begged. "Please don't."

"Laurie, it's not true. I'm not one of them. I had to use you, I had to make you shoot her. It was the only way. . . ."

The words didn't reach her. For a moment longer I knelt beside her trembling body on the sand, tasting the bitterness of her fear of me. Of me! I knew there was nothing I could say that would wipe away the memory of the dreadful whiplash of my own projected thoughts.

I stood up. She shrank further away from me. I turned to stare at the blackened crystal fragment, at the shapeless heap of dust beside it, washed now by the incoming tide. I felt no sense of triumph. In the end it was not I who had won. The alien had been destroyed by an ordinary, frightened human being.

The thought startled me. I confronted it with growing wonder. I had used the phrase automatically: an ordinary human being. And what was I? A thing to be feared. A step beyond.

I too was an alien mind.

In that moment I was conscious of a new aloneness. For years, I had known an isolation from the world around me. I had walked apart, and the sense of exile had walked with me, not understood, beyond any experience that would have allowed me to understand it. And now I knew at last the thing which made me different, like the impulse which had driven the first feeble-legged creature from the sea to walk apart upon the land.

I turned back to Laurie. For a moment longer I stared at her. Slowly, I bent to pick up the gun she had dropped. The movement made me wince as pain shot through me from the stiff, scorched fingers of my left hand. They felt

152

as if the flame still burned upon them. They smelled of smoking flesh. I set my teeth against the pain. Without a word, I turned my back on the girl's frightened eyes and walked back down the slope of the beach.

The blackened crystal glittered wet. I picked it up. A dead piece of rock. Frozen matter. Nothing. I took it with me. It seemed fitting that the two aliens should meet once more, the one who had died—and the one who lived.

24

ALL THE OFFICES in the Science building were dark. The corridors glowed with a glassy, empty brightness. Behind me the campus was dark and deserted. I tried the main doors. They were locked. I had started to turn away when a thought struck me. I stared at the lock. Concentrating on it, I tried to see the naked mechanism. I thought of a key turning, of the tumblers dropping, of the click of the opening lock. Sweat broke out on my forehead. I bent the full weight of my mind upon the resisting sliver of metal. It clicked.

For a moment I leaned against the door. I was near a state of total exhaustion. The pain in my hand now was almost unbearable. I had wrapped a handkerchief around it. Charred flesh had stuck to the cloth.

When I looked up a watchman was moving along the corridor directly toward me. I ducked back out of sight. I felt neither surprise nor satisfaction over the power I had just discovered. After waiting a moment, I edged forward and peered through the glass in the door. The watchman was not in sight.

I went in through the unlocked door. My steps sounded loud on the hard polished surface of the corridor. As I reached the office door, the watchman's footsteps thudded on the stairs nearby, descending with a weary, deliberate tread. Apprehensively, I twisted the handle of the door. It was locked. My new trick worked on this door, too. The watchman's legs were visible on the staircase as I slipped into the dark room, not daring to close the door completely for fear of the noise it would make.

I stood tense behind it, waiting and listening. I heard the low quick catch of my own breath and felt the fluttering heartbeat of excitement. The watchman's steps shuffled past the door. They stopped. Through the glass panel I saw the shadow of an arm reaching out. The door opened part way. Standing behind it, holding my breath, I heard the watchman grunt. He pulled the door shut with a decisive bang.

I waited a moment before checking the door. It had an automatic lock which was now set.

When I was sure the watchman was out of earshot, I searched the office and its connecting laboratory. Both were empty. I went back to the desk in the office and took the black crystal from my pocket. I set it on a sheet of paper in the center of the desk top. Turning away, I brushed my burned hand against the edge of the desk. A sheet of pain shot up my arm. I swayed dizzily, gritting my teeth. It seemed to take a long time for the pain to ebb. My heart thudded heavily.

As I crouched behind the door to wait, the first light of dawn sent thin streamers above the horizon. In the darkness of the room the black crystal on the desk seemed to have a glow from within. Its many facets caught and held the feeble light filtering through the opaque glass from the bright corridor. I thought of the thing's active state. I thought of viruses on earth which in their inanimate state had all the properties of ordinary rock crystals, responded to chemical experiments in a predictable way—until they touched the living organism on which they fed and thrived, became themselves living, breathing, growing parasites. I thought of a dead planet dotted with beautiful colored crystals. . . .

Slowly, the building came to life. Gray early morning light washed the office. Voices spoke nearby in the corridor and the sounds of movement whispered through the walls.

It seemed to me to be hours before firm steps approached the office door and halted. I felt too tired to move. A key turned in the lock.

Dr. Temple had taken no more than two steps into the room when he sensed my presence. He stopped in mid-stride. I slammed the door shut and stepped close behind him. He swung around slowly. I marveled at the iron discipline that kept him from showing surprise or shock. His face was expressionless, his eyes like pieces of polished blue slate. They were fixed on the muzzle of the gun I held inches away from his skull.

"You won't have time to stop me, Doctor," I said softly.

Only his eyes moved, shifting cautiously from the gun to my face. "What is the meaning of this?"

"You don't seem surprised to see me."

"I am too old for surprises."

"How old are you, Doctor—in human years, that is?"

He frowned, eyeing me speculatively. His gaze swiveled around the room.

"She's not here," I said.

"I don't know what you mean."

"I mean she's dead. I killed her."

He looked at me sharply. "You killed someone?"

"Not a person—but I killed the thing you see on your desk."

He spun toward the desk. I saw the bunching of his shoulder muscles under his jacket and my finger tensed, hovering against the trigger. The black crystal on the desk top winked with reflected light.

"And what is that supposed to be?"

"The alien, Doctor. I used a flame on it. It was the only thing I could think of that would be effective."

I thought the skin of his neck paled, but I couldn't be sure. Again I was struck by the degree of his self-control. But perhaps he has no emotions, I thought. Perhaps he doesn't feel anything at all—love or hate, excitement or fear. He might be able to analyze them coldly but he wouldn't understand them. The thought excited me. Here was a weakness in the alien mind.

"You are a sick man, Mr. Cameron," Dr. Temple said quietly. "I realized that you were ill when you talked to me on Saturday—but I did not then believe you capable of murder. If you've really killed someone you are in serious trouble. And you have also been hurt. Your hand—"

"I only need one good finger to kill you," I said. "I could have done it as you walked through the door but I wanted you to know it was coming."

He smiled thinly. "And why should you want to kill me?"

"Because you are one of them—the leader. I should have known it before, I guess. It wasn't until I saw the hardened crystal that I knew. That's how you got to earth, Doctor—as a pair of innocent-looking crystals. I don't pretend to understand what kind of creature you are but I've seen the other crystal there in both its frozen and its active states. I imagine you were the first one to be activated. The real Dr. Temple received the crystals for research. He was probably the first one to touch them with his bare hands—or his tongue."

"You have a vivid imagination, Mr. Cameron."

"Then all you had to do was find a suitable subject for the other crystal. Helen Darrow was a shrewd choice. She would never be suspected and she could work closely with you under the guise of a student."

"Helen Darrow?"

I laughed. "It's no good, Doctor. It won't work."

"I'm going to call a doctor for you, Mr. Cameron. I hope what you say about killing a girl is not true. But I'm afraid I shall also have to call the police."

For the first time I felt a twinge of doubt. His reactions were not what I had expected. But he had to be the other alien. It couldn't be anyone else.

He took a step away from me. "Don't move!" I snapped.

He froze. I pushed the muzzle of the gun hard against the back of his neck.

"If you do that again, I'll kill you!" I said savagely.

For a moment he was silent. Then he spoke quietly, his voice soothing like that of a parent talking to an offended child. "That will accomplish nothing except my pointless murder, Mr. Cameron. I will do all I can to help you. And I assure you that you will not be held responsible for the killing of this—this girl you say is dead. You are not of sound mind. I can testify to that and I'll be believed. My word carries a lot of weight."

"I'm sure it does. But you're not going to testify to anything. I'll think no more of destroying you than the other one. It will give me pleasure."

"You keep saying you killed one of these—these aliens of yours. Tell me, how did you succeed in doing it? Didn't you tell me they were able to control your mind? Surely the creature would have been able to stop you."

"She did stop me, Doctor—but I'd figured on that. I took precautions. I had someone else there with me—a girl. She had a gun. While the alien tried to make me drown myself, the girl got behind her unnoticed and shot her."

The scientist was silent for a moment. When he spoke his voice seemed harder, colder. "Clever, if true," he said. "But it surprises me that a bullet would destroy the hold this creature had on its body. If it was as powerful as you say it was, I would think—"

"Hope, you mean, don't you, Doctor? Are you still wondering whether a bullet would disturb your body? I think it will. I gambled on that and won. You'll lose control. There really isn't much of that body left, is there?"

"You should write fiction, Mr. Cameron. This is all very interesting, but since I'm not one of your aliens will you please remove that gun from my neck? It is not a pleasant feeling."

I hesitated. He hadn't introduced one false note. If he were not the alien I would be destroying one of the world's greatest men, an irreplaceable mind. But there was only one way of finding out. I had to make him act.

"I'm sorry, Doctor," I said. "I can't take any chances. And I've delayed too long. I have to kill you."

"You'll never get away—the shot will be heard."

"I'll have to run that risk."

My finger started to tighten on the trigger. My hand was shaking and my mouth was dry.

"Stop!"

The unleashed force of his mind was beyond any power I had yet experienced, crushing and terrible. My right hand was a thing of petrified wood, without nerve or feeling, incapable of the fractional pressure that would have sent a bullet smashing into the alien's brain.

"You force me to do this," he said harshly. "You are a stupid man."

I fought to open the constricted muscles of my throat. "You—you didn't think I'd come alone, did—did you?" I choked out.

He smiled. "That's a very old trick, Mr. Cameron. I am in full possession of Dr. Temple's memory so I cannot be fooled by your childish ruses. I'm perfectly aware that there is no one behind me. Coming alone was very foolish. You might have won."

He had to believe me. I had to break for an instant the unbearable pressure of the force that froze my hand. Then I realized that my burned hand could move. I controlled the first leap of excitement. He wouldn't believe I had an ally—unless he read my mind! If he felt the wild rush of my relief and excitement he would believe. And it wouldn't have to be relief—it could be any emotion! Any feeling at all! He wouldn't immediately know the difference!

And suddenly I looked past him. My eyes brightened with delight and a smile leaped to my lips. In that same instant, I scraped the raw, burned flesh of my left hand across the sharp-edged buckle of my belt. Pain stormed through my body and exploded in my brain—searing, hideous, heart-stopping pain. And the alien turned in frantic haste.

For a split-second I felt relief from the pressure of his

mind. My finger jabbed the trigger and the gun spat. A raw, black hole opened in his skull.

As he fell, I was already jamming the gun into my pocket and fumbling for the lighter. The sound of the shot had been loud in my ears, but I felt sure that it would have been only a muffled retort in the corridor. It might be another minute before anyone came to investigate. Or it might be seconds.

His face started to decompose. The coverall he wore began to sag as his body disintegrated before my eyes, no longer held together by the power of the alien mind, pulsating now in shrill, meaningless waves. I saw behind the powdery tissue a withdrawing tentacle of cells. Feet sounded in the corridor outside and there was a murmur of voices. Someone tried the door.

The alien shrank, the fingers folding inward, wrapped in the hardening membraneous tissue. I waited a moment longer. An urgent knock rattled the glass panel of the door. The singing vibrations dimmed in my mind like the fading wail of a siren.

And the glittering crystal lay still on the floor among the dust and the soft white bones and the crumpled coverall. I turned on the blue jet of flame and held it on the bright surface of the crystal chunk, held it while the coverall's smoking stench filled my nostrils, held it until the blackened face of death had seeped deep into the heart of the thing on the floor.

I heard voices through the haze in my brain. "Something's burning!" "Open up in there!" "Dr. Temple? Are you there?"

I scooped up the crystal chunk. It was still hot, but there was no life in it. I grabbed the other from the desk and jammed both into my pocket. Then I bundled the pile of soft, pulpy bones and decayed tissue in the folds of the coverall and threw the bundle into a wastebasket beside the desk. I grabbed a pile of papers and crammed them into the basket.

When the door was smashed inward I was heroically

trying to put out the fire which had somehow started in the wastebasket. I had burned my left hand badly in the process. There was nothing left of the man who had been Dr. Jonas Temple but a pile of smoking ash.

25

MORNING SUNLIGHT HAD dissipated the early mist. I walked slowly along the road from the elevated station toward my trailer. Behind me the night's nightmare, the hour of suspicious questioning about the fire. Someone had remembered my visit to Dr. Temple on Saturday, so my appearance there this morning had seemed plausible. There would be more questions, I knew, when Dr. Temple did not appear. I didn't care. There would be questions but no answers.

The two small crystal clusters felt heavy in my pocket. I stopped and took them out, weighing them in my hand like marbles. I had an impulse to throw them into the dust at the side of the road. Instead I pushed them back into my pocket.

Souvenirs, I thought. One needed to remember.

I looked up. A tall slim figure stood at the edge of the highway, her blonde hair shimmering in the sunlight. She began to run toward me. I couldn't move. I felt an elation I had never known before, a strange whispering excitement. And suddenly I knew what I must subconsciously have divined at the very beginning, knew the incredible truth. Here was more than a woman's suppliant beauty, so marvelously warm and human. Here now the reason for the shy withdrawal, the trembling eagerness, the intimate knowledge. Here was—

"Erika!"

The cry arrested her. She stopped not ten feet away from me, breathless. I felt the quivering of her unvoiced fear for me, the surge of joy that leaped into her mind.

Her mind!

I knew then that I had not called aloud.